Amberly

AND THE
SECRET OF THE FAIRY WARRIORS

GINA VALLANCE

FriesenPress

Suite 300 - 990 Fort St
Victoria, BC, V8V 3K2
Canada

www.friesenpress.com

ISBN
978-1-5255-8037-6 (Hardcover)
978-1-5255-8038-3 (Paperback)
978-1-5255-8039-0 (eBook)

1. JUVENILE FICTION, FANTASY & MAGIC

Distributed to the trade by The Ingram Book Company

To all my little cousins (and those who aren't so little anymore),
I dedicate this book to you. Remember: always believe in your
dreams—and never, ever give up! XOXO

Chapter One

"Aaaah! Cold! Cold!" Amberly cried out as she woke up to icy dew drops falling on top of her weary head. Instantly, the disheveled little Whimsical fairy jumped out of her tiny, duck-feathered bed. Her book, *The Secret of the Fairy Warriors*, which had been tucked safely beneath her tiny, peach-colored, paralyzed left wing, crashed to the floor with a loud thud. Amberly shook her head and brushed her damp red hair out of her groggy, sparkling-green eyes with her hand. Her normal-sized, healthy, reddish-orange right wing fluttered.

As she held onto the side of her bed to keep her balance, Amberly slowly bent down and picked her book up off the floor. Her Uncle Orin was Whimsical Land's fairy sorcerer. Once a fairy warrior himself, he had given Amberly the book when he learned how determined she was to someday become a fairy warrior herself to find her father.

Amberly's father's name was Foster, which means "guardian of the forest." Foster had disappeared from Whimsical Land when Amberly was just two years old. She was certain that if her mother, Orla, would just let her take sword-fighting lessons with Uncle Orin, she could fight whatever evil had taken Foster from Orla and Amberly and Amberly's sister Calista. But, unfortunately, as far as Amberly's mother was concerned, having a paralyzed wing and bad balance made sword-fighting lessons completely out of the question.

"Up and at 'em! Hurry up, Amberly, or you will be late again!" said Safflower, a tiny but tough fairy butterfly. Safflower, who was

Amberly's "watcher," fluttered her tiny purplish pink wings. In order to wake Amberly up every morning, she had come up with this new, awful ritual of pouring icy dew drops onto Amberly's head from her handmade twine and tree sap mug.

"Ok, ok! I'm up! I'm up!" said Amberly as she stood upright, balancing herself next to her bed. She fluttered her large, healthy right wing even faster now. She had been so startled by the cold water that she thought there might have been a tinge of feeling in her paralyzed left wing, even though she knew that it was impossible.

Amberly despised her crippled wing. It was vastly smaller than her right one and it didn't work one bit. It was paralyzed—stiff—useless. With just one healthy wing, the only way Amberly could run, glide above ground, and land upright was by using her running stick. Since she was unable to fly, she used her running stick to catapult herself through the air. Then she used it for balance, so that she was able to land on her feet without toppling over. Without the running stick, Amberly's larger wing would have pulled her straight down to the ground due to the uneven weight of her wings.

As a younger whimsy, cuts and bruises had been the norm for Amberly until her mother had given her the strong stick made of cedar. To make the apparatus even more appealing, Amberly's big sister, Calista, had carved beautiful shapes of flowers, vines, and fairy wings onto the thick wooden stick. They made Amberly smile. Calista had even carved a message onto the stick, which read, "To my sister: You are my strong, beautiful hero and don't you forget it! Love Calista."

Amberly needed to protect her head as well, so her mother made her a tiny helmet out of an acorn shell that she insisted Amberly wear. Amberly definitely didn't love the homemade helmet, but she grew used to it and the little helmet quickly became a part of her.

"Up all night reading again?" said Safflower.

"Uh huh…"

Amberly yawned sleepily as she held on tightly to *The Secret of the Fairy Warriors* while she balanced herself. Standing in one place and walking slowly weren't the issue. However, running, jumping in the air, or any fast movement using her arms was impossible without using her running stick to lean on. She used her left hand for her running stick, so this meant she could only use her right hand to lift things. If she didn't have her running stick at a given moment, she held on to anything in close proximity to prevent herself from toppling over and falling to the ground.

"You must get your rest at night, Amberly! You'll have no energy to run and leap the way you do!" Safflower said.

"I always have energy…Once I'm up that is," said Amberly as she rubbed her eyes.

Amberly watched Safflower quickly fly over to her small wooden closet and open its little blue doors, which were beautifully decorated with hand-painted celestial-yellow suns above each of the two doorknobs.

Amberly stood with her book in her arms. She stared at her open closet, focusing on the handmade fairy-warrior outfit that was hanging in its place. It was practically calling out to her with a voice of its own saying, *Let's go! Adventures are to be had, Amberly!*

A hopeful fairy warrior at heart, Amberly dusted off her incandescent, healthy right wing with her hand. This wing, which had sprouted out from behind her right shoulder when she was a newborn fairy, was always illuminated with a beautiful, orange and red hue and felt just like satiny spider silk.

She then forced her attention onto her tiny, stock-still, paralyzed wing, which was no bigger than a toddler's fairy wing, and sported the color of a faded peach. This tiny, paralyzed wing seemed to have a personality all its own. Amberly imagined her little sallow wing having a face. In her mind, that face stared back at her with shame-filled, droopy eyes, desperately trying to hold back its tears. At the mere thought, Amberly abruptly looked away.

She shook off her ugly thought, set the book down on her nightstand next to her father's small, hand-painted portrait, walked toward her closet, and opened it. Swiftly, she retrieved her handmade fairy-warrior garb, which consisted of a white peasant blouse, a green corset, brown arm bracers made of tree bark, forest-green tights, and a brown belt with an emblem on the buckle in the shape of a beautiful, gold, fairy wing. Standing upright on Amberly's closet floor were her dark-brown boots decorated with tiny, amber stones.

To top off her fairy-warrior attire was the brown, leather-strapped scabbard that she wore across her back every day. It was really made for holding a sword; however, she was forced to use it to hold her running stick, since she was not allowed to use the scimitar sword Uncle Orin had given her.

Whenever she leapt into the air for a few minutes, Amberly placed her running stick in her tube-like scabbard, then she pulled it back out when she landed running, in order to balance herself. She just could not wait for the day that she didn't need her running stick, so she could carry her sword in the scabbard like a real fairy warrior.

Hanging on the back wall of Amberly's closet hung her scimitar sword, covered by its black leather sheath. Amberly slowly glided her hand over her prized procession. Unfortunately, taking her sword out of her room or even removing it from her closet for that matter, had been forbidden by her mother.

Rapidly fluttering her wings, Safflower brought Amberly the white peasant blouse with her tiny black appendages. Amberly quickly walked behind her changing curtain and traded her nightgown for it. She slipped her arms through the blouse's sleeves then put on her green corset over her blouse. Safflower happily helped tie the corset's laces in front.

Next, Safflower tossed Amberly her arm bracers and Amberly slid them onto her arms. She slipped into her green leggings and then secured her fairy-wing-designed belt around her waist. Lastly, Safflower brought Amberly's boots to her with a sense of urgency.

Safflower looked so tiny as she flapped her wings fiercely while her little black appendages tightly held onto Amberly's heavy boots.

Safflower was abnormally strong for a fairy butterfly just as Amberly was for a Whimsical fairy. Even though fairy butterflies were much smaller than Whimsical fairies, between the two of them, Amberly and Safflower were stronger than a pack of wolf pups running in the moonlight.

Although it looked like Safflower was helping Amberly transform herself into the fairy warrior she hoped to become, the reality was that Amberly's mother had forbidden her to take sword fighting lessons with Uncle Orin. Amberly tried her best to not give up hope that her mother would one day change her mind.

Just as Safflower set Amberly's boots down in front of her, Amberly decided to jump into them instead of putting them on one by one. She saved herself from falling by grabbing onto her changing curtain, practically ripping the whole curtain off its brass pole. Safflower flew over to Amberly's running stick in the corner of her room, wrapped her appendages around the long stick, and started to fly toward Amberly.

Amberly ignored Safflower and like a flash of lightning, pulled her scimitar sword from its hook and slipped off its sheath. As soon as she uncovered her sword, she felt a kind of strength within her. Her legs felt as if little sparks of energy had ignited her muscles.

In a flash, Amberly began to run and leap around her room, catching herself from falling while trying to balance. Her body swayed side to side each time she landed on the floor. When she jumped in the air once again and then fell onto her knees with a thud next to her bed, Safflower could do nothing but watch in horror.

"Amberly! Stop that!" said Safflower as she flew closer to Amberly with the running stick. She fluttered in place, waiting patiently for Amberly to take the stick from her.

Amberly completely ignored Safflower. With great speed and excitement, she summersaulted over her bed, sword in hand. She landed on one knee and then jumped over her small cedar desk, accidentally knocking over Safflower's mug and a full pencil holder.

Amberly fell straight to the floor, landing on her side next to the mug and fairy pencils that were now scattered about. She forced herself up onto her feet while Safflower fluttered nervously around her. While leaning against her bed, with one swift move of her wrist, Amberly tossed the sword into the air, caught it, and then stabbed her pillow with it. Duck feathers burst from her pillow and flew everywhere. She and Safflower watched in awe as a few duck feathers landed on her nightstand around her father's portrait.

"I'm going to find you no matter what it takes. I promise you that," Amberly said softly to her father's portrait. She picked up the portrait and placed it in her burlap satchel bag. Hoisting the bag's strap over her head, she adjusted the strap snugly over her left shoulder and across her chest.

Suddenly, her trance like state was interrupted.

"Amberly! What is going on in there?" her mother called out with concern. It was time for Amberly to leave for her fairy pollination-training class. She knew her mother must have been patiently waiting for her to eat breakfast. Amberly rarely sat and ate breakfast; however, her mother never gave up trying to make her start.

"Coming, Mother!"

"I hope you are not sword fighting in your room!"

"No, I'm not!" Amberly said guiltily. With Safflower at her heels, she quickly placed her sword back on its hook.

Safflower quickly nudged Amberly's side with her running stick. "Take it! Look how much you hurt yourself without it!" she said. She stared at Amberly's wrist, which was red from Amberly having fallen on it.

"I'm fine, Safflower. I hate that thing! How can I ever learn to sword fight and become a fairy warrior if I have to use this stupid running stick!" Amberly shouted as she angrily grabbed the running stick from Safflower's long appendages.

"Your mother is right. It's not safe for you to handle a sword when you lose your balance so easily. It's dangerous! Look at your wrist. It's red. Does it hurt?"

Amberly rolled her eyes. "No, it doesn't hurt. I'm fine!" With that, she strapped her acorn helmet onto her head and ran out of her bedroom using her running stick.

Safflower flew closely behind her.

The little fairy kitchen smelled of roasted nuts and some sort of delicious broth. Standing in front of a little potbelly stove was Orla, Amberly's mother. Orla's grandiose, burgundy wings fluttered about nervously while her long, silky, black hair blew gracefully in the wind they created. She was pouring toasted nuts from a little pan into a small, white-cotton bag with a draw string. Suddenly Amberly ran into the kitchen with her running stick, leapt in the air, summersaulted, and landed right in front of her mother.

Orla was startled but she handed Amberly the white little bag filled with nuts and laughed. "Oh, Amberly Crimson. What am I going to do with you?"

"Do about what?" Amberly asked as she put the little bag of nuts in her brown, over-the-shoulder satchel bag.

"Never mind. You'd better run along. You'll be late," said Orla.

Amberly smiled, gave her mother a kiss on the cheek, and then leapt across the kitchen toward the door like a whirlwind. This caused her mother's hanging copper pots to clatter and fall.

"Bye Mother!" shouted Amberly as she ran out of the fairy cottage.

"Goodbye!" Orla shouted out of the open front door as she waved. "And don't forget about the next Fairy Wedding Day rehearsal! You have to be there for your sister this time!"

"I know, Mother! I knooooow!" Amberly yelled. Her voice echoed in the wind. She was running and leaping so fast that she was already at the end of her fairy cottage's cobblestone walkway and about to disappear into the lush forest.

Orla shook her head and sighed as she closed the red, white-spotted, teardrop- shaped fairy door.

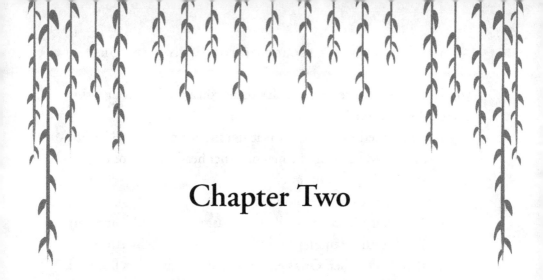

Chapter Two

"Hey! Wait up!" shouted Safflower.

Amberly looked back at her little fairy butterfly and slowed down so that Safflower could land on her shoulder.

Safflower held on for dear life as Amberly ran and leapt into the air. She glanced back at Amberly's fairy cottage and could barely see Orla, who was waving from the window. She and Amberly were already half a mile away from home and the crisp cool air felt luxurious as it brushed against their cheeks.

Running with great speed, Amberly catapulted through the air with her running stick and then landed firmly on the ground. She was running and gliding so fast into the lush forest that the elm trees and shrubs looked like a blur as she whizzed by.

Safflower shrieked and laughed out loud at their speed.

As Amberly ran and leapt through the air, she thought about the dance rehearsal for the fairy wedding day, which was only three weeks away. Her big sister Calista would be getting married alongside thirty other fairy couples. Calista had just turned twenty years old and she was so excited to marry Drake, her true love. Amberly was happy for her big sis, and she really did like Drake, but she wasn't looking forward to the fairy wedding dance that she was to be a part of. When it came to dancing, Amberly had two left wings as well as two left feet. Running, jumping, and rescuing wounded animals she could handle, but dancing? Amberly?

This wasn't the only reason she hated being a part of Fairy Wedding Day. Another reason had been weighing heavily on her mind as well.

"Wow! You're really getting good with using your running stick, Amberly!" said Safflower as Amberly finally slowed down and began walking through the shrubs and trees.

"Thanks, Safflower. You know what else I think I'm good at?"

"Eating chocolate-covered berries?" Safflower asked with a laugh.

"No, silly."

"What?"

"The fairy wedding dance."

"I'm sorry?...What?" Safflower said with a gulp.

Amberly tried to hold in her laughter. She knew this was definitely not the truth but she continued to state her case anyway. "Yeah, I think I'll be fine. I really don't need to go to the rehearsal."

"Ooh no you don't. Nope. You're not getting out of it this time!" Safflower said. Her voice became a little panicked. "You're going. I promised your mother you'd be there!"

Frustrated, Amberly jumped into the air. Pretending it was a sword, she used her running stick to swat off a thin branch hanging from an old evergreen tree.

"Why don't you want to go, Amberly? You really could use the practice, you know?"

"Hey!" Amberly said. She was trying to hide her hurt feelings even though deep down she knew it was true. She believed that one day she would be great with a sword, but dancing? Not so much.

Amberly sighed as she walked briskly through the forest while Safflower fluttered and flew as fast as she could to keep up with her. Once the fairy butterfly had caught up, Amberly noticed Safflower's intense little stare as she fluttered above her head. Safflower was clearly waiting for an explanation that Amberly really wasn't in the mood to give. Still, she knew she had to say something, or else Safflower would never let it go. "Safflower, you of all those closest to me should know why I hate fairy wedding day!"

"Hmm…Can I just have a hint?"

"Safflower! How can you forget my cousin, Nissa?"

Safflower gasped and fluttered around Amberly's head in a nervous tizzy. "Oh dear! I…I could never forget about poor Nissa! The tragedy of it!"

Amberly walked between some mossy little mounds and pebbles, and then started to gain a little speed. Safflower knew this was her cue to land on Amberly's shoulder and hold on. In a flash, Amberly began running as fast as she could while Safflower did her best to hang on.

After Amberly summersaulted over bushels and stones, she finally landed on her feet. Imagining it was a sword again, she swatted at the air with her running stick while trying to get the memory of what had happened to her fairy cousin out of her mind.

"Do you think she's with your father?" Safflower asked curiously.

"Yes, I'm sure of it. When we lost her on Fairy Wedding Day, I just knew that whatever happened to her and the other missing Whimsical fairies also happened to my father," said Amberly sadly. "It was the Nyxie Fairies that took them. I just know it."

As the legend goes, the band of Nyxies lived in the Dark Forest according to Amberly's book, *The Secret of the Fairy Warriors*. The Nyxies were drawn to the natural energy source within the Whimsical fairies' colorful wings, especially when one was flying alone. The Nyxies were known to use the Whimsicals' wing energy and pixie dust to enhance their magic.

As she ran through the forest at lightning speed, Amberly tried not to think about the fairy wedding dance too much. She loved the sound the wind created as she zipped passed the trees and catapulted herself with her running stick over shrubs and ponds. Sometimes, she could glide for a few minutes at a time in the air if she ran and catapulted herself with just enough force.

She was going to be late for fairy pollination class…again. She really didn't know why it mattered, though, since she always got her pollination magic assignments done faster than any of the other young fairies. Her big sister, Calista, knew this as well, which is why she didn't get angry about Amberly being late to class. Luckily for Amberly, Calista was her fairy pollination teacher, which Amberly loved. It was Corliss, Calista's snobbish friend and assistant teacher, who always made a fuss when Amberly was late. Amberly just ignored Corliss, though. Corliss hated when Amberly ignored her, but Corliss was one fairy who just couldn't keep her mind on her own two wings!

Speaking of wings, Amberly tried one last leap and glide just before she made it to the wildflower training patch, up ahead. This was the place where all of the young fairies would learn to super-charge the natural pollination process by shaking the magic pixie dust off of their wings as they flew over the wildflowers before the bees came to pollinate. Between the whimsical fairies' magic and the bees, the wildflowers would bloom into the most beautiful flowers one had ever seen.

Still running and leaping through the air, Amberly passed a few willow trees. With Safflower still holding on tightly to her shoulder, she gained more speed and leapt over a running stream. But she tripped and fell head-first on top of a log, bounced off of it, and then landed flat on her stomach in a mound of green, wet, moss. Her running stick somehow became lodged between two stones on the other side of the stream. Thankfully, her little acorn helmet had protected her head. "Ouch!" she yelled.

"Are you ok?" shouted Safflower, who had taken cover between Amberly's shoulder and her scabbard's leather strap.

"I'm fine," said Amberly as she used her running stick to help pull herself up off the ground and stand upright. With Safflower still holding on, Amberly started running again and then rolled into a quick summersault just before she landed on the soft grassy hill leading to the large wildflower pollination training patch.

In the distance, Amberly saw Corliss leaning over and talking into Calista's ear. Amberly had exquisite hearing. "Leave my sister alone!" she heard her sister say. Amberly loved when her big sister stood up for her. She stood tall and then ran over the grassy hill.

When she ran fast enough, Amberly could sometimes make the ground shake. As she entered the wildflower patch, her feet made the ground rumble so hard that the flowers began to shiver and shake from the force of her running feet. By now, everyone knew Amberly had arrived. The shaking was a strange phenomenon that they had all gotten used to. It was so embarrassing to Amberly though. *I'm a fairy, not a troll,* she thought to herself as the ground rumbled below her feet. Nevertheless, most of the fairies were always happy to see her, despite their laughter.

The other fairy students watched Amberly as she raced through the entrance to the pollination training flower patch. She catapulted herself high above the flowers and the other fairy students who were flying low to the ground while shaking their magic pixie dust off of their wings and onto the wildflowers' pistils.

As Amberly leapt high into the air, she fluttered her wings and shook off her own pixie dust from her healthy right wing over the wildflowers. Then she saw Calista hovering below her. Amberly jumped right over Calista and rustled her sister's soft, curly brown hair with her hand. "Hi sis!" she said. When she landed, her running stick sunk deep into the soft, damp soil. She fell backward and ended up in a sitting position beside her sister.

"Hi love. You all right?" said Calista as she fluttered her periwinkle blue wings.

Embarrassed, Amberly stood up and brushed herself off. "Why do I always end up falling to the ground? I'm a fairy not a troll!" she shouted as a few of the other fairies giggled behind her back.

"Don't say that, Amberly! Being different isn't a curse. You should be proud of your strength and speed. After all, it's our unique abilities that can save us when we least expect it," Calista said as she gently patted her little sister's back.

"How can I save anyone, especially Father, if I have to use this stick forever! I hate it!"

"That stick helps you leap and run faster that any fairy can fly, little sis! If you didn't have it, you wouldn't be able to run and jump the way you do. Who cares if it interferes with your landings once in a while? That's why you have this!" said Calista as she knocked on the top of Amberly's acorn helmet with her curled fist and smiled.

"But, I'm the only fairy in the world that can't fly. It's not normal!" shouted Amberly.

"You may not be able to fly, Amberly, but look how strong you are, instead! You're stronger than all of us. You can lift anything!"

"But fairies don't need to be strong! We need to be able to fly!"

"Oh, yeah? And what about the animals you rescue with your strong arms when you pull apart those metal traps that those poor creatures get caught in? You don't need to fly to do that!"

Amberly just shrugged and looked down at the ground.

Calista nudged her arm and pointed into the air at Safflower. "Hey, what's with her?" she said.

Amberly and Calista both started laughing out loud as they watched Safflower twirl in the air while fluttering her little wings. She was mimicking Amberly by performing her own summersaults. She was doing a pretty good job—for a fairy butterfly that is.

"Woohoo! Look out beloooow!!" Safflower screamed while she distracted the other fairies, who were spreading their magic pollination pixie dust over the wildflowers. Safflower was so busy watching the other fairies that she wasn't paying attention to where she was going and accidentally bumped right into Corliss's head.

"Ouch! Safflower, watch it!"

"Oops! Sorry!" Safflower shouted with a giggle.

Amberly could hardly contain herself as she tried not to explode with laughter. Poor little Safflower could be somewhat clumsy, but her clumsiness did come in handy at the best times! Amberly laughed to herself as she ran and leapt in the air while shaking her magic pollination pixie dust off her wing. The red-orange, sparkly dust floated down slowly and covered the wildflowers as she flew over them. She was almost done with her quota when she quickly landed, ran on the ground, zigzagged in between the flowers and then leapt high above the wildflower patch while spreading more of her magic dust. She landed back on the ground right in front of her fairy friend Spice.

"Hi Amberly!" said Spice. Now that they were older, Spice's gorgeous, shiny-black hair had become longer and thicker. Her skin was the color of cocoa and her wings were a shimmery, light pink. She looked beautiful in her pink pixie dress and she was still as sweet as she was when she had been a little whimsy. Spice was a fast talker and bubbly as ever.

"Hi Spice!" said Amberly.

Spice sat down next to Amberly. "Whew! I really could use a break! How are you? How's the fairy warrior book? Are you still reading it?"

"It's good, I…"

Spice interrupted with excitement. "Any clues yet about where your father might be?"

"Well, no, not…"

"Hey, just ignore Corliss, she's just jealous of you, ya know?" said Spice in a hurry.

Amberly could barely get a word in edgewise with Spice, but Spice had such a warm heart. "Thanks, Spice."

"No problem. I always got your wings, you know. I…I mean… wing…aww…you know what I mean."

"Yeah, I get it," Amberly said with a smile.

Spice smiled back and glanced at Amberly's little paralyzed wing. Something behind Amberly suddenly made her frown.

Amberly turned to see just what had landed behind her and to her misfortune, it was the horrible twins with their large, blue wings; black, wavy hair; and their muscular, bare chests that puffed out like proud roosters. These boy fairies thought they were Whimsical Land's princes but little did they know, no fairy in Whimsical Land could stand their very presence, including Amberly.

"Hey, look! It's the fairy with the stump for a wing. Aww...too bad you have to run instead of fly," said Javyn, who smiled devilishly with his crooked and cracked front teeth.

"Leave her alone, Javyn!" said Spice. Spice was so angry that you could almost see steam flying out of her ears.

"What's it to you, slow poke?" said Razi, Javyn's twin brother who suddenly moved closer to Spice.

Amberly stared at the boy fairies angrily, but she could never find the right words to say whenever Razi and Javyn said or did something horribly mean to her or her friend Spice. Her throat would seem to close and her voice would suddenly stop working.

"Hey! Leave her alone, Javyn!" shouted little Safflower as she hovered over Spice.

"Move along!" Razi said as he swatted Safflower away with his hand. His fingers barely touched Safflower but the force of his hand made her fall to the ground. Javyn and Razi started laughing like hyenas at poor Safflower.

"Hey!!" Amberly shouted and ran toward Razi, using her running stick to help her gain even more speed. She stopped just inches away from his face. The twin brothers stopped laughing in an instant. By now, some of the other fairies had gathered around Amberly and Razi, and some were peeking out from behind the wildflowers' stems as they whispered to each other. Amberly could see all the fairies out of the corner of her eye. Their little wings looked like swirls of blues, purples, oranges, reds, blues, and greens as they fluttered them with great speed between the flower stems. Amberly scooped Safflower up off the ground, set her tiny fairy butterfly on her shoulder, and stared angrily at Razi. Her lips were curled in a snarl and her eyes squinted with fury. Safflower was just as fearless and angry as Amberly.

"What? Cat got your tongue again?" Razi said with a smirk.

Amberly was thinking of kicking Razi all the way to the grassy hill when she heard Calista calling out to her. Lucky for Amberly, her big sis was always there just when she needed her.

"Amberly! It's not worth it!" Calista shouted as she flew over to Amberly and grabbed her little sister's arm.

Without a word, Amberly quickly turned her back on Razi and diverted her eyes toward Safflower, who was still sitting quietly on her shoulder. "Let's go" Amberly said to her trusted butterfly.

"And where are you going? To get that wing of yours fixed?" Javyn said with an evil smirk. "Oh, wait, I forgot. That thing can't be fixed!" He slapped Amberly's running stick with his hand and knocked it to the ground.

Did he really just do that? thought Amberly. The all-encompassing rage she felt at that moment, from the top of her head to the tip of her toes, was immeasurable. Although it was impossible, she could almost feel her paralyzed wing twitch. Amberly was on fire now and she couldn't hold back. She snatched up her running stick and like a lightning bolt, she twirled around and used its bottom end to toss mud right smack in Javyn's face.

The cruel troll of a fairy ran into the nearby stream to rinse out his eyes.

Amberly was out of breath as she stared at Javyn running toward the stream. *What have I done?*

To Amberly's surprise, loud cheers emerged from all the fairies who had been hiding in between the flower stems.

"Go Amberly!" said a young boy fairy.

"Way to go!" said a petite fairy with long blonde hair. Her smile made Amberly want to hug the sweet little fairy and she almost burst into tears.

"Amberly! Oh my! Let's go!" said Safflower, who fluttered her wings nervously.

Calista put her arms around Amberly protectively as she glared at Razi, who was still standing nearby.

"You better not have ruined his eyes!" yelled Razi.

Amberly was startled by Razi's harsh accusation and tears began to well up in her eyes. "I didn't mean to…"

Calista suddenly interrupted Amberly in mid-sentence. "Enough!" she screamed in a raging fury. "Listen up! Amberly will always be stronger and faster than any of us! The sooner you realize that, the less chance you both have of getting hurt!"

Razi finally backed down and flew toward his brother, who was still rinsing his eyes out in the stream.

"Come on, Safflower," said Amberly.

"Yes, ma'am! Where we goin?"

"Away."

"Be careful, Amberly. And don't forget about the fairy wedding rehearsal!" Calista said with a little worry in her voice.

"I know…I know," Amberly said with a forced smile. All Amberly could do now was think about getting back to her fairy warrior studies and off she ran with Safflower on her shoulder.

Calista watched her little sister with great pride as Amberly ran and leapt with great speed in the distance. Even though Amberly wasn't perfect, and neither was anyone else for that matter, Calista only wished Amberly could see herself the way she saw her, which was as nothing short of a miracle.

Chapter Three

Safflower held on tightly to Amberly's shoulder with her strong little extremities while Amberly ran and leapt high in the air, and then glided forward for short distances at a time before landing on her feet. She landed so hard this time that if it hadn't been for her running stick to help her balance, she would have fallen flat on her face. She had to admit that she was grateful for this helpful apparatus, even though she hated that she had to use it.

Amberly sighed a sigh of relief and was looking forward to her favorite part of the day, which was reading *The Secret of the Fairy Warriors* in solitude. As she catapulted above the shrubs and mossy ground a few feet at a time, she steered her little vessel of a body with her healthy wing. Zigzagging between the evergreen trees, she headed for her favorite reading spot. The humans called it the "Major Oak," and it bordered Whimsical Land's woods and Sherwood Forest. Amberly could hardly wait to climb up the Major Oak and settle into the little abandoned nest that rested on its top branch. She had claimed the empty nest months after the last baby bird it had housed flew away. Before that, a human and his group of friends had used the Major Oak tree as a hideaway. Robin Hood they called him. He was the leader of his other human friends and they always seemed rather…merry. The first time Amberly had seen the Major Oak tree she couldn't wait for Robin Hood and his merry men to leave. They were usually there every morning and every afternoon. But when there was no one in sight, she climbed up the tree and used the nest as her little reading nook.

The Major Oak tree was Amberly's sanctuary. *Ahh...finally!* she thought, as she climbed up to the highest branch where the cozy nest sat. How her legs longed for a rest as she sighed with relief and lowered her weary body into the soft nest lined with feathers and fuzz. Safflower hopped off of Amberly's shoulder and rested in the nest beside her. It was the perfect spot for Amberly to study and for Safflower to nap and rest her tiny fairy butterfly wings.

Amberly opened her fairy warrior book and concentrated on each page with her entire being. As she focused on every word, she imagined herself a seasoned fairy warrior, mastering the skills she would need to fight off whatever evil had taken her father.

A few hours passed by as Amberly eagerly devoured each chapter of her book while basking in the sunlight. She loved being surrounded by the peaceful sound of the forest's birds chirping in harmony, and she was utterly lost in her own world until she was startled by a loud whimsy voice.

"Amberly? Amberly? Come out, come out, wherever you are!"

Amberly set her book down and looked toward the ground below. *How could they have known about my secret hiding place!*

Flying between the shrubs below were three little whimsies. One was Bliss, a little whimsy fairy with gold curls and powdered blue wings that matched her fairy dress. Bliss's whimsy friends were flying right behind her.

Avery must have told them! Amberly thought to herself. Her best friend Avery had found her in the nest one afternoon, but he'd promised he wouldn't tell a soul. *But Bliss isn't supposed to be so far from home.*

Amberly looked on as Bliss's little fairy friend Coral, who sported peach-colored hair, an orange dress, and white fairy wings flew after Bliss. So did their friend, Remi, a mischievous, fun-loving, little-boy fairy with deep-green hair, lime green eyes, forest green wings, and tan skin. Coral and Remi followed along with whatever Bliss did.

Amberly stayed quiet as she as watched the little ones search for her.

"We're going to find you!" said Coral, who flew in circles with her peach hair bouncing above her shoulders and her wings fluttering as fast as they possibly could.

Amberly went back to reading her book and figured the little whimsies would probably search all day for her and not even think to look up at the top of the tree where she and Safflower rested in the nest.

She had a strong feeling that little Remi would not give up, so Amberly stopped reading for a moment and grinned as she watched Remi below. He was searching behind bushes now and scratching his head, trying desperately to find her. He stopped for a moment and brushed his green hair out of his eyes just as Bliss rushed up behind him.

"Boo!" shouted Bliss, causing Remi to fly straight up in the air. Little Bliss had this relentless habit of scaring Remi to no end.

"Hey! Knock it off!" Remi yelled as he flew around nervously.

Amberly giggled to herself and realized her studying time was probably over now, even though it seemed as though it had just begun. She didn't think the little whimsies would leave unless she made an appearance. So, she put her book back in her satchel and quietly climbed out of the nest. The little whimsies were now huddled around the bottom of the Major Oak's trunk as they bickered with one other about which one of them would most likely find Amberly first.

"I say...None of you will be the first to find me!" Amberly blurted out as she jumped off the lowest branch on the tree and landed right in the middle of the three little whimsies. Safflower flew down right after her.

"Amberly!" Bliss squealed with delight.

Amberly laughed as Bliss flew up to her shoulders and embraced her neck with a warm hug while Coral and Remi hugged her leg. They were all so much shorter than Amberly since they were just five fairy-years old.

"How did you find me?" Amberly asked.

The three little whimsies stared at Amberly with guilty faces.

"Avery..." said Remi.

"I knew it. Well, you whimsies know when I go into the woods by myself it's for an important reason, right?"

"Yes, Amberly, but..."

"But what, Bliss?" snapped Amberly.

Bliss took a step backward. The embarrassment in her eyes suddenly broke Amberly's heart, even though she couldn't help the way she felt. "You aren't even supposed to be this far away from home, Bliss. You'll get in trouble!"

"Sorry, Amberly," said Bliss as she took Coral by the hand.

"We didn't mean to bother you," said Coral. Her little eyes looked as though they were about to fill up with tears, while Amberly once again, felt like a selfish little imp.

Bliss kicked a stone and stared at Amberly sadly.

"Well, now I feel like a real snot! All right...It's ok," said Amberly as she tickled little Coral until she could hardly control her laughter anymore. Bliss, Remi, and Safflower flew around Amberly and Coral while they all began to laugh.

Amberly picked up Bliss and threw her high into the air. Bliss laughed hysterically as she flew above the trees. The whimsies loved Amberly's strength because they could never fly very high unless Amberly threw them up toward the clouds.

"I want to do that!" said Remi.

"Ok, are you sure you're ready for this?" Amberly said with a grin.

Remi nodded and smiled nervously.

"Me too! Me too!" shouted Coral.

"Well, all right. If you're sure!" Amberly said to Coral as she held Remi by the waist. Remi looked up at Bliss, who was still floating high above them in the air. "You ready?" Amberly asked him and he nodded yes.

"On three!"

"Ok!" Remi said with a giggle.

"1...2...3!" Amberly threw Remi up in the air and he soared above the trees with little Bliss. Then Amberly grabbed Coral by the waist and lifted her up. "On three, ok?" she said.

Coral nodded her head excitedly. She couldn't wait to join her other two friends high in the air.

"One, two, three!" Amberly said loudly as she tossed little Coral into the air.

Coral let out a long scream then laughed along with Bliss and Remi as they all three floated through the air just below the clouds.

"Wow!" said Safflower. "Hey! Be careful up there! Amberly, you sure they will be able to come back down?"

"Of course, they will, Safflower!" said Amberly, who was slightly annoyed.

She was suddenly startled by a deep voice in her ear. "You think they can handle it?"

Amberly turned around abruptly and saw Avery standing behind her. He fluttered his wings and smiled flirtatiously. Amberly rolled her eyes and Avery just stared back at her and gave her a wink.

"Avery! How did you know what time I'd be here?" she asked.

"Fairies have the best eyes and ears, you know. And don't forget the ability to be incredibly silent investigators," said Avery with a laugh. Giving Amberly another wink he sat down on an old log in front of him. Casually, he glanced up to the sky and pointed at Bliss, Coral, and Remi, who were still floating high in the air just below the clouds. "How will they make it back down?"

Amberly sat down beside him on the log. "They'll come down. When they're tired, they'll just stop fluttering their wings, and I'll catch them. They know the routine."

Avery put his arm around Amberly and grinned. Amberly didn't know what had gotten into him ever since he'd turned thirteen. She really missed the old Avery. The two had grown up together and when they were little whimsies, they loved playing fairy ball, fairy racing games, and embarking on forest scavenger hunts together. They played so well together and had so much fun growing up, and now, he just made things well, kind of...weird.

"Knock it off, silly," Amberly said as she shoved his arm off her shoulder.

Avery just laughed. He was used to Amberly shooting down his advances, but he tried his best to get her attention anyway. By this time, the whimsies were beginning to come down full force, headed straight for them. Amberly nudged Avery and prepared herself for catching them.

"Get ready! Amberly said to Avery, who stood at attention. He was just as eager to catch the whimsies as they fell closer and closer to the ground.

Bliss laughed nervously as she headed straight for Amberly. "Amberly! Here I come!" she shouted.

Amberly caught her with one swoop of her arms. "Woah! You're getting a little heavy, Bliss!"

"I'm going to be six this year!" Bliss said as Amberly set her down on the ground and patted her head.

"Look out!" Avery shouted as he jumped in front of Amberly just in time to catch Remi in one arm and Coral in the other.

"Ahhh!" Remi yelled and then laughed hysterically as Avery set him down.

"Yay!" screamed Coral. The two were thrilled and greatly relieved to be caught. The little ones always came down with such speed, just like shooting stars.

"Thanks Avery!" said Coral.

"That was fairy cool!" Remi said as he laughed and gave Avery a little fairy high five.

"Nice flying, whimsies," Avery said kindly.

The little whimsies laughed and ran around the Major Oak's trunk and started a game of fairy tag. Amberly watched them for a moment and thought about how much she and Avery had loved playing together when they themselves were just little whimsies.

She felt Avery staring at her now and she turned around only to find him sitting down on the log again.

"Hey, come here for a sec," he said with a smile as he tapped the empty space beside him.

Amberly looked at him and then shifted her attention to the path behind her that led to home.

"Come on, just for one second," pleaded Avery.

"Oh, all right. But only for one second," Amberly sighed and sat down next to Avery with Safflower resting on her shoulder.

Avery smiled with relief and stared at Amberly for a moment.

"So…What's up?" asked Amberly.

"Nothing. Can we talk?"

"Sure," said Amberly.

"I miss my best friend," Avery said sincerely.

"Oh…well, I'm here now. What do you want to talk about?" Amberly said with sincerity, despite trying to fight the urge to get up and delve back into her book.

Avery reached into his brown trouser pocket and pulled out three mini, red rosebuds. He smiled and held them in front of Amberly.

Amberly didn't know why but she was startled by his sweet gesture. As sweet as it was, she did not respond very kindly. "What's that for?" she said to Avery as she swatted his shoulder, causing him to fall off the old log and land right on his back.

"Hey! What's wrong with you, Amberly?"

Amberly looked down at Avery, feeling guilt and anger at the same time. "I…I'm sorry," she said and offered her hand to help him up onto his feet.

"It's ok," said Avery pulling leaves out of his chestnut-brown hair as his turquoise wings fluttered slowly. "That's why I love you."

"Ok, umm…I gotta go," said Amberly uncomfortably.

"No, no, wait!" said Avery.

"No, really. Fairy Wedding Day rehearsals are today. I gotta go!"

"But, Amberly! Wait!" he said desperately.

But by now, Amberly's mind was completely made up. She grabbed Bliss, who had just begun to run circles around her, picked her up, wrapped her arms around her, and hugged her tight. "See you later, Bliss!"

"Aww! Bummer," said Bliss.

"Bye whimsies!" said Amberly as she started to run.

"Bye whimsies!" Safflower shouted as she held on tight to Amberly's shoulder.

"But, Amberly!" Avery called out.

"Sorry, Avery! Maybe I'll see you tomorrow!" shouted Amberly. And with that, she leapt into the air and headed for the Fairy Wedding Day dance rehearsal.

Chapter Four

Amberly continued to run and leap swiftly through the lush green forest. Safflower laughed as she sat on Amberly's shoulder and held on. Just a mile to go and the two would be at the fairy wedding rehearsal with a forced smile on Amberly's face.

The ground rumbled from the force of Amberly's feet as she ran toward the grassy hilltop. This is where Calista, the other fairy brides, bridesmaids, fairy grooms, and groomsmen were practicing for the fairy wedding dance.

"Amberly!" Calista shouted.

Amberly was surround by a huge dust ball that had followed her after she ran through a dry dirt patch. She ran as fast as she could and summersaulted right up to Calista, stopping inches away from her sister's face just as the dust cleared. Leaning on her running stick she stared into her sister's stressed-out face.

"Amberly! You're a mess!" Calista said with disdain.

Amberly was embarrassed as she brushed the dust off her tights and blouse. "Sorry," she said awkwardly.

"You're late!" Calista said as she tugged at Amberly's arm and pulled her toward Seth, Amberly's dance partner.

Seth wasn't very bright but he was a nice boy fairy. He stood in the long line of the other fairy groomsmen and faced Amberly. The fairy grooms and groomsmen, and fairy brides and bridesmaids were lined up in two perfect rows facing each other as their purple, blue, pink, orange, yellow, and burgundy wings fluttered in unison.

Amberly stood stiffly in front of Seth. He smiled shyly as he fluttered his teal-colored wings and blinked his big brown eyes nervously.

"Go get 'em tiger!" Calista said to Seth as she gave him a wink. He blushed bashfully. Amberly rolled her eyes and gave Safflower an agitated glance out of sheer embarrassment. Safflower quickly flew off and rested on a bed of wildflowers where she had the perfect front row seat for their dance performance.

"Let's just get this over with," said Amberly as she took hold of Seth's hands. As long as she held his hands, she could keep her running stick snug in her scabbard.

Seth nodded in agreement and the music began. The fairy brides began to dance with their fairy groomsmen as their beautiful smiles gleamed from beneath their soft veils made of spider silk.

"It's our turn!" Amberly shouted. She really didn't mean to say it so loud. Everyone was looking at her now. She really should have just given Seth the cue by blinking her eyes like she and Seth had planned, but of course, that's not what happened. *Oh well*, Amberly thought to herself as Seth pulled her closer to him.

Seth knew not to let Amberly go or she would definitely fall. As the two began to spin around the fairy brides and their bridegrooms, who had formed their own dancing circle amongst themselves, the melody took on a faster pace. Amberly could hardly control her feet! Her feet were moving so fast as Seth twirled her around, he could hardly keep up with her. As he continued to spin Amberly while holding her hand above her head, she felt as though she was about to fly away at any moment.

As Amberly spun around, Seth was supposed to dance around her, but Amberly held on to his hand so tightly now that it began to turn blue. She couldn't slow down! She accidentally tugged Seth's hand so hard that it slipped from her grip. The mere force of Amberly's strength made Seth fly sideways into the other groomsmen dancing next to them.

"Oh no!" Amberly screamed as Seth tumbled sideways through the air. He became so dizzy from the force at which Amberly had accidentally thrown him, he was unable to fly high enough above everyone and he flew right into one of the groomsmen's back, causing that groomsman to bump the next poor fairy groom next to him. This caused a ripple effect of falling fairy groomsmen. One by one they toppled over.

"Sorry!" Amberly said to Seth, who was on the ground rubbing his head.

"Amberly!" Calista yelled at her so loud that Amberly flinched.

She hated when her sister yelled at her. It was so annoying and unnecessary. "I didn't meant to…"

Calista had fury in her eyes. "Amberly, you need to pay attention! Can't you focus on anything other than your stupid fairy warrior book for once?"

"What do you mean my stupid warrior book? You know I can't dance!" Amberly retorted.

Calista dusted off Seth while the others staggered back to their dancing positions. "Nothing else matters to you except your stupid fairy warrior book!" she yelled with her face turning redder and redder by the second. "Just go, Amberly. Who am I kidding? I should have never asked my kid fairy sister to be my fairy bridesmaid." Her face was cold.

Tears welled up in Amberly's eyes. She had never seen Calista look so disappointed and hurt. "Calista, I'm sorry. I'm just not good at this kind of stuff!"

Calista leaned closer to Amberly. Her eyes were on fire now. "If you hadn't missed so many rehearsals, you'd be fine!"

"I—I'm sorry," Amberly said with shame.

"Forget it. Just go read your fairy warrior book, Amberly."

"But…"

"Just go!" Calista stared at Amberly for a moment teary-eyed and then turned and walked back to her fairy groom.

The music started again and Amberly couldn't help but feel utterly alone. Safflower suddenly came to the rescue and sat on her shoulder.

"Come on, Safflower..." Amberly said sadly. Her little fairy butterfly companion nodded her head. Amberly wanted so badly to run as far away from the fairy wedding rehearsal as possible, but she just couldn't. She didn't have the energy, so she began to walk. She concentrated on walking, one foot in front of the other with the help of her running stick, which now had become a walking stick. Her tears flowed freely down her cheeks. The cool wind took over and dried her tears for her. Her heart felt heavy and her legs were beginning to slow down. Even the sky looked sad as it began to turn grey. Amberly felt so exhausted that she stopped to sit beneath a willow tree a distance apart from the fairy wedding rehearsal. She sighed as the music played louder.

Amberly watched the fairies dance from a far and thought that maybe if she watched them dance for a little while, she would be more prepared for the next fairy wedding dance rehearsal. "Calista couldn't have really meant those mean things she said, Safflower," she said softly.

"Of course not! She's just a stressed-out fairy bride-to-be right now," said Safflower.

"Well, maybe If I did focus even more on learning from *The Secret of the Fairy Warriors* and convinced Mother to let me take sword fighting lessons with Uncle Orin sooner, I'd be able to find our father before Calista's Fairy Wedding Day! I know how much she misses him. Just think how happy she'd be, Safflower!"

With a loud swoosh, Razi flew down from the top of the willow tree and came crashing down clumsily, landing right in front of Amberly. "Found ya!" he said with a mischievous laugh.

"Lovely," Amberly said, unenthused.

With another thud, Javyn landed right beside his brother. "Fancy meeting you here," he said as he glared at Amberly.

Amberly just ignored Javyn. She looked away and tried to act as if he weren't there.

"What's the matter, Amberly. Cat got your tongue again?" said Razi as he laughed obnoxiously.

Amberly gave Razi a quick, icy stare and then looked away uncomfortably. How she wished she could really say what she felt, but something inside always seemed to stop her. She felt as though she had a monster inside of her made of pure fear that always managed to silence her voice.

"Get out of here! Find your own tree!" Safflower yelled at the top of her tiny lungs as she hovered above Amberly's head protectively.

Razi backed up and then slipped, causing him to fall to the to the ground.

"You misfits need to leave!" shouted Safflower while Amberly held tightly onto her running stick and was preparing herself to flee.

"Ooh, I'm shaking!" Javyn said defiantly.

Razi just laughed at his brother and nudged him. "Come on Javyn, let Amberly sit here and cry since she has nothing better to do."

"Yeah, if she can't fly, what else is there?" Javyn said with a smug look on his face. His little smirk disappeared as soon as he caught a glance of the angry look on Amberly's face.

Amberly rushed toward him and stared him right in the eyes. He backed up a little. Her lips were quivering. She tried to open her mouth to speak but, her words escaped her again and she silently turned to walk away.

Safflower quickly flew off Amberly's shoulder and headed straight for Javyn. "Amberly can run circles around you, Javyn!" she shouted. "She's faster than you will ever be! She's going to be a fairy warrior! You just wait and see!"

Javyn let out a quiet laugh. "Yeah, right. Her? A fairy warrior? Ha! What kind of fairy warrior doesn't fly?"

"A very fast one!" Safflower shouted.

"I *will* be a fairy warrior and I *will* find my father!" said Amberly.

"Ha!" Javyn laughed. "You think your father mysteriously vanished? Well, he didn't. He *made* himself disappear because he couldn't handle the embarrassment!"

"My father would never just leave! He had nothing to be embarrassed of!" said Amberly.

"Oh yeah? How about a fairy daughter that can't fly? Sounds pretty embarrassing to me," said Javyn with a laugh.

Consumed with anger, Safflower flew toward Javyn. She slammed into his shoulder so hard that he tumbled backward and fell right on his behind.

"Hey!" he shouted.

"You stupid little imp!" yelled Razi as Safflower quickly flew back toward Amberly and landed on her shoulder. Razi gave Amberly and Safflower an icy stare.

Amberly knew in her heart that Javyn and Razi were just jealous that she could run faster than they could fly. But she couldn't help but feel hurt by Javyn's cruelty. She took a step back and was at a loss for words.

"Your father didn't just disappear, Amberly. He was ashamed of you, so he left!" shouted Javyn.

Safflower gasped at the hurtful words that had spilled out of Javyn's mouth.

Amberly just stared into Javyn's hateful eyes. Her thoughts were spiraling out of control in her mind. Memories of her father flashed before her eyes. *Could he really have been ashamed and embarrassed of me?* She remembered the moment when her father had sadly stared at her when he first realized her left wing didn't work. The sadness in his eyes at that moment had haunted her for years. Just when she had finally forgotten that memory, Javyn brought it back to the surface.

Safflower broke Amberly out of her trance when she began yelling at Javyn, demanding that he leave Amberly alone. Without even realizing what she was doing, Amberly jumped in the air, causing Safflower to hold on tightly to her shoulder. Then Amberly ran as fast as she could, far away from Javyn and Razi.

Chapter Five

The front door to the little fairy cottage flew open as Amberly ran inside. She obliviously rushed right passed her mother, who was sitting quietly in her fluffy living room chair sewing a long, beautiful, emerald-green dress accented with gold lace. The spools of thread that had been perfectly stacked on top of the little table beside Orla toppled over and fell to the ground as Amberly whizzed by like a whirlwind.

"Mother? Mother?" Amberly shouted from the back hallway that led to her mother's bedroom.

"I'm right here, Amberly!" Orla shouted back as she calmly picked up her spools of thread off the floor.

Amberly ran back into the living room and stood in front of her mother. She was completely out of breath as she stared at the unfinished velvety-green dress in her mother's lap.

"What do you think?" asked Orla.

Amberly sighed and plopped herself down on the fluffy blue sofa across from her mother. "It's gorgeous," she said quietly.

"I can't wait to see you in it on Fairy Wedding Day! Your sister is going to be so proud of you!"

Amberly sighed as a wave of despair made its way across her face. Her eyes welled up with tears as she leaned back into the soft sofa. She closed her eyes and felt as though she wanted to disappear.

"Amberly? Amberly what's wrong?"

Amberly took a deep breath and slowly opened her eyes. She stared at her mother for a moment.

Orla leaned forward and stared back at her fairy daughter with concern. Since Foster's disappearance, the light in Orla's eyes had seemed to grow dimmer with each passing year. Soon, Amberly was afraid her mother's eyes might darken so much that they would become like little black orbs protruding from her pale, fair skin, which is why Amberly just had to find Foster.

"Did something happen at fairy wedding rehearsal?" her mother asked.

Amberly released a slow sigh and put her head in her hands.

"Amberly! What is it?" Orla stood up, made her way to the sofa, and sat down next to Amberly. She gently pulled Amberly's hands away from her face and Amberly looked at her mother sadly. Safflower, who had been sitting on the back of Orla's chair looked on sadly too.

"Amberly, you really need to learn to speak up. What's wrong?"

Amberly took a deep breath and dried her eyes. "I know the truth about father."

"The truth? What truth?" Orla asked curiously.

"I know why he left."

Orla stiffened and her heart skipped a beat. She stared at Amberly and tried to blink back her tears. "What in the world are you talking about?"

Amberly took a deep breath and stared sadly into her mother's eyes. "Father wasn't kidnapped. He…he left because he was ashamed."

"Ashamed? Ashamed of what?" Orla said with the kind of concern only a mother could feel.

"Of me!" Amberly shouted.

Orla's eyes widened and she took Amberly in her arms and hugged her tight. "Oh, dear one, what gave you that idea?"

Amberly slowly pulled away from her mother's embrace. "Well, Javyn said that…"

"Javyn!" Orla shouted. "Why on earth would you listen to that bullying fairy? I thought I told you to stay away from him and his weasel of a brother."

"I try but he always seems to find me. He said he heard from the elder fairies that father was ashamed that his fairy daughter couldn't fly, so he left. All this time, Mother. All this time I thought he had been kidnapped by the band of Nyxies from the Dark Forest and you let me believe that!"

Orla sighed and took Amberly's hands into her own. "Amberly, listen to me. The truth is, when your father saw that you were unable to fly when you were just a little whimsy fairy, he did leave."

Amberly gasped and put her head in her hands, letting out a small cry.

"No, no! Let me finish!" Orla said as she pulled Amberly's hands away from her face. "He left because he wanted to help you. He loved you so much. He wanted to find a cure. A magic cure."

"Magic? But you always said Father hated all magic except for natural pixie dust magic."

"You're right, Amberly. He believed that magic should only be used for the benefit of nature by helping flowers and plants flourish. But, for you, he was willing to try anything, which is why he left."

"But, where was he going, Mother?" Amberly asked with desperation.

Orla sighed and squeezed Amberly's hand. "When your father left, he said he was going to seek help from your Uncle Orin."

"Uncle Orin? No, my uncle would have told me this."

"He didn't want to upset you, Amberly, which is why he has never mentioned it. Your father was in search of a spell or anything that could heal your paralyzed wing. Uncle Orin is the most gifted fairy sorcerer in Whimsical Land and your father knew it even if he didn't believe in using magic for the benefit of fairies. He did it because he loved you, Amberly."

Amberly slowly pulled her hand from her mother's grip. "But, why haven't you told me this before? After all this time, Mother!"

Safflower flew from Orla's chair where she had been resting, and landed on the back of the sofa behind Amberly. She looked at Orla with concerned eyes.

Amberly directed her attention over to Safflower. "And you? You knew this too?"

Safflower stared at Amberly with guilt in her eyes.

"I don't understand. Why didn't anyone tell me this?"

"Amberly, sweetie, It just never seemed like the right time. We didn't want to upset you."

"I was already upset, Mother. Javyn was right. I *am* the reason Father's gone!"

Orla hugged Amberly and held her close. "It's not your fault, Amberly. Don't ever say that again!"

"Tell me what happened the day I was supposed to fly in the First Flight Festival. I want to know everything."

Orla nodded her head and took a deep breath. "Ok, Amberly. You're right. It's time you knew the whole story."

Amberly stared at her mother attentively. She was focused on her every word.

"It was the day of the First Flight Festival when every two-year-old whimsy fairy was supposed to take their first fairy flights," Orla said with a slight smile while fighting back the tears in her eyes.

Amberly sighed and sank back into the sofa as she prepared herself for the story that she knew was going to change her entire life forever.

Chapter Six

The First Flight Festival always took place in the spring. Springtime in Whimsical Land was the most beautiful time of the year. It was the season that birthed the most colorful wildflowers. Blue, red, and purple petals always dazzled in the sunlight. The gorgeous flowers were the result of all the hard work the young fairies had performed while pixie dusting every new crop of wildflowers.

Deep within the woodlands of Whimsical Land stood a cobblestone stage that was surrounded by eager fairy parents who were waiting for their toddler fairies to fly on their own. It was a Whimsical fairy ritual that happened every spring, and every spring the same announcer, named Pauper, a handsome, flamboyant male fairy with bright pink and blue wings, blond hair, and grey eyes announced the "First Fairy Flight" countdown. Pauper had always been the performer in Amberly's little fairy village. It was he who was in charge of the countdown when Amberly was just a little whimsy.

As Amberly's mother continued to share her memories of Amberly's First Flight Festival, Amberly swore she sensed a vague memory in her mind of Pauper's very distinct, high-pitched voice.

"Ten, nine, eight…!" Pauper shouted as he continued the countdown. After he finally counted down to one, the fairy toddlers who were extremely excited and eager to fly, unraveled their wings by themselves.

Foster held little Amberly up toward the sky. His eyes stayed focused on his fairy daughter as he waited patiently for her wings to unravel from the two tight, little wing rolls on her back. Orla described this moment in such wonderful detail that Amberly felt as though she could almost remember this moment herself.

The entire audience full of Whimsical fairy parents waited with great anticipation while the crackling sound of one hundred toddler fairy wings slowly unraveling echoed throughout the forest. Gasps of joy could be heard all around as fairy parents marveled at their little ones' wings.

Orla and Foster were still eagerly awaiting the unraveling of their whimsy daughter's wings; however, it was Amberly's misfortune that her wings did not unravel like the others.

The other fairy toddlers began to flutter their wings at the same time. Amberly's memory of this part of her life had faded, but as her mother told it, her wings unraveled very slowly. Her right wing stretched out to a reasonable size and glistened in the sunlight with a golden orange and red hue. As for her left wing, well that was a different story. It was tiny and stiff. There was no getting it to move. Amberly's healthy wing fluttered slowly at first then took on a standard momentum, but since the other one was paralyzed, she was unable to fly like the other whimsies.

Orla recalled the moment when all the other toddler whimsies flew above their heads. She remembered Amberly focusing on Foster, whose watery big green eyes were locked on Amberly. He did not cry, but Orla could still see the image of his face, heartbroken, and sorrowful when he realized…his daughter could not take flight.

Standing in front of an elm tree behind Orla, and Foster, was Orin, Orla's older brother. Orin had long grey hair, bright blue eyes, and bluish grey wings. According to Orla, Foster had the utmost disdain for Amberly's Uncle Orin. Foster had never been keen on the idea of Amberly's uncle being a fairy sorcerer. He didn't believe in using magic for the purpose of benefitting fairies and Orla had always told Amberly this ever since she was a whimsy.

"Our magic is meant to assist the flourishing of nature," he would say. So, it was no surprise when Foster's anger flared up the moment Amberly's Uncle Orin tried his magic on Amberly's paralyzed wing.

Just as a rainbow of color made up of small, fluttering, toddler fairy wings blanketed the sky, Orin put his hand on Amberly's paralyzed wing. His eyes began to glow with a yellow hue and a strange, bright, glittery gold beam of light glided from his eyes onto Amberly's paralyzed little wing. As the light disappeared and Uncle Orin's eyes reverted to normal, he sighed and sadly shook his head. It was no use. His magic didn't work on her unavailing wing. Orin frowned and held his little whimsy niece's feet in his hands. Then his frown began to fade and he let out a loud, joyful laugh.

When Amberly asked her mother why her Uncle Orin had laughed, her mother's answer shocked her.

Orla told Amberly that her uncle was overjoyed because, after his magic had failed, he'd had a vision of Amberly's future. "He said you would have strong legs that would be capable of gaining greater speed than if you could fly," Orla said with a smile. "He knew you were special, Amberly."

Given Foster's disapproval of Uncle Orin's use of magic, in a fury, Foster scooped up Amberly's big sister Calista in his arms and hoisted her on to his back. Her long, curly brown hair bounced freely, while her periwinkle blue wings fluttered about as she held onto their father's back. Foster despised spells, and in that moment, he wrapped one arm around Orla's waist as she held baby Amberly tight, and he flew off with his fairy family of four like a flash of lightning.

As her mother told the story, Amberly could almost remember how the cold wind had felt on her face while she was still nestled in her mother's arms.

Orla's memory of that flight was mixed with warmth and a slight fear, given the speed at which Foster had flown at that time. As Orla recalled holding little Amberly tightly to her chest, she remembered the feeling of Amberly's heart beating against her chest and she was comforted by the tiny heart's quick rhythm. Bum...Bum...Bum...Bum.

The four soared high above the trees toward their fairy cottage. It wasn't a long trip since Foster's wings were so large. When his wings were outstretched, he could be easily mistaken for a baby hawk. It was a wonder that no human had ever spotted him due to those unusually large wings.

Orla's embrace made little Amberly's fear melt away. Orla could usually make Foster's anger dissipate in seconds with her gentle touch, too; however, this moment was not one of those moments as Foster soared through the sky while carrying his fairy wife and daughters.

Later that evening, after Foster had calmed and Orla's nerves settled, little Amberly's fairy family sat at their wooden kitchen table. Amberly's big sister, Calista, eagerly grabbed a handful of the chocolate-covered berries that Orla had set on the table even though they were meant for dessert. One by one, Calista stuffed one round, chocolate-covered berry into her mouth at a time and handed a few to little Amberly. Calista laughed out loud when she noticed little Amberly sitting in her fairy highchair with melted chocolate all over her face.

As her mother continued the story, Amberly could almost recall the feeling of the sticky chocolate that had stuck on the corners of her mouth and vaguely recalled her mother wiping her face off with a warm cloth.

The laughter faded and Foster and Calista sat with long faces at their little kitchen table in front of their empty soup bowls. After Orla had finished pouring berry soup into all their bowls, little Amberly suddenly pulled out her pink sparkle toy ball made of pixie dust, moss, and tree sap, which had been wedged behind her back and her highchair. With sudden force, little Amberly threw the sparkly ball against the kitchen's wood-planked wall. It hit the wall so hard that it flattened upon impact and stuck there like a gooey, sparkling blob.

Amberly laughed when her mother told her this part of her memory of that day and she vaguely remembered feeling an insanely strong urge to throw objects and run like crazy when she was just a whimsy toddler. She imagined how startled her parents must have been when her little pink sparkle ball suddenly whooshed by their heads.

Orla recalled how little Amberly couldn't help but giggle just like any other normal two-year-old whimsy would have done. Later that night, little Amberly was still full of energy and threw one of the living room oak chairs across the room with one hand. With the other, she picked up her mother's music box from the fairy-wing designed coffee table and threw it across the room as well! After having travelled at full speed, the music box crashed and shattered against the floor.

It was then that little Amberly had discovered her strange and astounding strength, and she suddenly had this uncontrollable urge to run as if her entire life depended on it. She ran so fast around the living room and kitchen while her parents and Calista sat dumbfounded. Then, she ran halfway up the wall, kicked off, summersaulted, and landed perfectly on her feet.

Orla recalled how little Amberly laughed so hard that she almost lost her breath, and that suddenly, she'd had the urge to run straight toward her parents, who were still sitting at the table with their eyes wide open. During this time as a little whimsy, Amberly's wings were both the same size, so nothing interfered with her balance. That all tragically changed as Amberly grew older and her healthy wing grew much larger than her paralyzed one.

Amberly landed perfectly on her father's shoulders after somersaulting in the air, giving him the opportunity to yank her right off his shoulders.

He quickly sat her down on the table in front of him. "Amberly! What on earth?" Foster said sternly. Little Amberly just smiled and clapped her hands. Foster looked at Orla with confusion. He set Amberly down on the floor and she immediately started to race around the room again while her parents went on to discuss her Uncle

Orin's magic, and the newly discovered, incredible strength Amberly now had in her legs and arms.

Little Amberly couldn't stop running and jumping over the sofa and chairs while her big sister eagerly tried to catch her. Amberly's laughter was so loud it made her parents stop their bickering and Foster and Orla both let out a loud gasp as they looked up toward the section of the ceiling that Calista was pointing to. Hanging on to one of the wood planks in the high ceiling was little Amberly.

"Amberly!" Orla cried out.

"Mama!" Amberly shouted out to Orla with a giggle. Before Amberly could even blink, Foster flew up to the ceiling and took her in his arms, and little Amberly was back on the ground before she knew it.

"That's it! I'm going to see Orin!" Foster said sternly. Calista and Amberly watched their mother and father argue as Orla insisted that her brother Orin had nothing to do with Amberly's sudden strength and speed. It was in that moment that Orla told Foster the details about Orin's vision of little Amberly's future. That's when Foster decided to go to Orin's cottage and talk to him about this vision he'd had of little Amberly's legs being faster and her arms being stronger than those of any fairy with healthy wings.

Even though Orla begged him not to go on a journey to Orin's late at night, there was no convincing Foster. He insisted Orla stay with Calista and Amberly.

Orla recalled that he thought the forest was no place for a speed racing, summersaulting, toddler fairy. "He said you were too fast for us, Amberly. He thought that you could have easily gotten hurt since you didn't know your own strength."

Amberly couldn't recall her father kissing her on the top of her head as her mother said he did, but she vaguely remembered her big sister hiding her face in their father's neck, sobbing softly after he had picked her up.

The sweet moment came to an end, and Foster walked right out of the front door. Orla set little Amberly down, and Calista and Amberly ran to the window. They both watched their brave and determined father fly away. Amberly didn't know why she and her sister were so upset at the time, since Foster was only supposed to be gone a few hours. It was as if they knew in their hearts something their mother didn't—and that something was the reality that their father was not going to return.

The next morning after their father had left, Calista woke little Amberly up and helped her out of her bed of tweed and duck feathers. Amberly held Calista's hand as they sleepily walked into their parents' room. Orla looked like an angel, lying on her stomach with the bright sun shining on her pale face and red lips. As she slept, her flowing black hair was draped all around her velvety burgundy wings. Amberly and Calista tip-toed toward their mother, but their clumsy footsteps woke her right up.

Orla's wings started to flutter as her eyes slowly opened. She focused on the two little fairy whimsies standing before her.

"Where's Daddy?" Calista asked their mother.

Orla quickly sat up and glided her hand over the empty space beside her. "Foster? Foster?" she cried out. In a flash, she flew out of the room, into Amberly's bedroom, then Calista's bedroom, and then around the living room.

By then little Amberly was running after her, calling out to her father with Calista trailing behind her. "Papa! Papa!" the two shouted.

He was gone. He hadn't come home all night, which terrified Orla, who suddenly flew back into Amberly's bedroom, and grabbed an empty butterfly cocoon carrier with a red satin cord attached to it. Orla tied the cocoon carrier around her waist and quickly slipped little Amberly inside it. Safflower, who at the time, had just became little Amberly's watcher, flew over to the cocoon carrier and snuggled inside beside Amberly's paralyzed wing.

In a flash, the four were flying out of their fairy cottage door, with Amberly snug in her cocoon carrier and Calista riding on their mother's back. Orla frantically flew through the forest. Amberly stayed calm and warm while snuggled in her cocoon carrier, with her bouncy red hair flowing in the wind and her green eyes open wide with her new watcher, Safflower beside her.

Then, that peaceful moment was suddenly interrupted by a swarm of sadness when Amberly heard her mother call out her father's name as she frantically flew. "Foster! Foster!" Orla screamed.

Calista called out to him, too. "Papa! Papa!" she yelled with her little voice. Between feeling her mother's and sister's sadness as well as her own, little Amberly's tears finally escaped and rolled down her cheeks.

Safflower quickly made her way toward Amberly's cheek. "Aww... Don't cry. Do you know what time it is? It's butterfly kisses time!" Safflower said as she fluttered her tiny wings against Amberly's cheek. Little Amberly giggled because it tickled so much and the more Amberly laughed, the more Safflower tickled her with her soft, powdery wing.

Amberly's giggles suddenly came to a halt when her mother stopped abruptly in mid-air, fluttered in place, and then flew in circles so fast it made Amberly dizzy, while Safflower held on to her for dear life.

"Close your eyes, Amberly!" said Safflower. Amberly closed her eyes tight, but she could still feel the spinning sensation while she heard her mother's voice cry out, "Foster!!!!!!!"

That was the last time Amberly's mother said her father's name out loud. As the years passed, there was still no sign of Foster. Each night Orla lit a candle for him that she had made from beeswax. She had made the candle so large that it was almost as tall as her. It had lasted all these years and it still to this day, smelled of fresh raspberries. The ruby-red beeswax candle stood just a few inches tall now and it wouldn't be long before it completely melted away.

Amberly and Calista were always so hopeful that their father would come home. Each night after dinner, Orla saved whatever was left over from dinner for him, like pollen soup, berry souffle, or sunflower seed casserole. However, time continued to fly by, and the minutes turned into hours, the hours turned into weeks, and before they knew it, the weeks turned into years.

While the memories of Amberly's father stayed tucked away in Amberly's heart, life went on, and as nature would have it, Amberly and her sister continued to grow older. With each birthday that passed, Amberly's healthy wing grew at a normal rate but her paralyzed one continued to stay the same tiny size.

Chapter Seven

Amberly finally took a deep breath after her mother finished telling her the story of her First Flight Festival and her father's disappearance. She pressed her back into the blue sofa, closed her eyes for a moment, and sighed.

Orla stared patiently at her daughter and waited for Amberly to speak. When she realized that Amberly was not going to utter a word any time soon, she took Amberly's hand into her own. "You see honey? It wasn't your fault. He didn't leave because he was ashamed of you!"

Amberly looked into her mother's eyes as she fought back her own tears. She looked as though the life had been sucked right out of her. "But…It was my fault. He left because he wanted to fix this stupid, ugly, wing…"

Amberly looked over her left shoulder at her paralyzed wing and began to tug at it. She wanted so badly to rip it right off her back. She screamed and cried as she tugged at the wing, "I hate this stupid wing! I hate it!"

"Amberly! Stop!" Orla shouted as she pulled Amberly's grip from her tiny wing. She let out a gasp when she noticed a trickle of blood dribbling down the edge of Amberly's wing where Amberly had tugged at it.

Orla quickly grabbed a piece of cotton from her sewing kit and placed it on Amberly's bleeding wing. "Why would you do that, Amberly?" she shouted.

Amberly looked down at the floor for a moment. She suddenly felt ashamed of what she had done. She took a deep breath before she spoke. "I need to take sword fighting lessons, Mother," she said quietly.

"What?" Orla asked. "Amberly, you know how I feel about that. We've gone over this so many times. I…"

Amberly suddenly looked her mother straight in the eye and screamed so loud her mother and Safflower both jumped with a start. "It's my fault that he's gone and I need to take sword fighting lessons, Mother!"

A loud gasp escaped from Orla's lips. "I don't understand this obsession you have with all this sword fighting business, Amberly!"

Amberly threw her hands up in the air, then grabbed her *Secret of the Fairy Warriors* book from her satchel bag. "I'm not obsessed, Mother! I'm studying!" she said as she held up the book.

"Studying what?" her mother asked.

"I'm studying to become a fairy warrior of course! Haven't you've been paying any attention?"

Orla blinked her eyes and stared at Amberly curiously. "You…you want to be an actual fairy warrior?"

Amberly nodded her head.

"Oh, for fairies sakes, Amberly! Whatever for?"

"So that I can rescue Father! That's what for! And I can't do it without taking sword fighting lessons! Uncle Orin promised he'd teach me once you say it's ok!"

Orla shook her head and glanced at Safflower, who shrugged as she sat on Amberly's shoulder.

"Amberly what do you think you are going to rescue him from? We have no idea where he even is!"

"But I do! I do know where he is, Mother!"

Orla gasped and was silent for a moment. A sight glimmer of hope suddenly lit up her eyes. "You know where he is?"

Amberly nodded.

"Where?" Orla asked curiously. Amberly quickly opened her *Secret of the Fairy Warriors* book to the page showing a map. She placed the book on her mother's lap and pointed at the map. "He's here. In the Dark Forest!"

"What?" Orla said as she stared at the map in confusion and then looked into her daughter's eyes. "Amberly, sweetie. This isn't real. This is all a made-up story. Why on earth would you think your father was in this made-up land?"

Amberly shook her head sharply. "No! It's not made up, Mother! The Nyxie fairies in the Dark Forest have kidnapped Father! I just know it!"

"Nyxie fairies from the Dark Forest? Oh, Amberly. Even if the Nyxies from the Dark Forest existed, why would they want your father?"

"Well, according to the *Secret of the Fairy Warriors*," Amberly said with conviction as she set her book on her lap, "The Nyxies want to steal the Whimsical fairies' pixie dust because our pixie dust makes things grow. According to the legend, flowers, berries, fruits, and nuts don't grow in the Dark Forest, so the Nyxies want to steal our pixie pollination dust and use it to make everything in the Dark Forest grow. But, I have to find the portal. Uncle Orin said that the way to the Dark Forest opening is a mystery, but I know that one day I'll find it."

"Orin? Orla snapped. "Your Uncle Orin is the one putting all these ideas in your head? Did he give you this book?"

Amberly nodded with hesitation. "Yes, but these aren't just ideas, Mother. The Nyxie Fairies and the Dark Forest are real!" she said as she closed the book and held it closely to her chest. "Please, Mother. I need to take sword fighting lessons, so I can save Father once I find the Dark Forest!"

Orla stood up abruptly and gave Amberly a stern look. Amberly could feel her mother's stare burn right through her. "Amberly, I forbid you to take sword fighting lessons and that's final!"

Amberly quickly jumped to her feet. "But mother, please!" she shouted as she pulled her running stick out of her scabbard and rebalanced to keep herself from falling after jumping up so fast.

"I said no and that's final!"

"But why?" Amberly retorted.

"Amberly, you can barely keep your balance without holding on to your running stick even as we speak! How can you handle a sword? You can't hold on to your running stick and a sword at the same time!"

"I...I could do it! I'll figure it out!"

"Amberly, if something were to happen to you, I couldn't bear it! Now, just go to your room! I'm done discussing this!" Orla said sternly.

Amberly desperately tried to fight back her tears. "But Mother," she replied sadly.

"Go to your room, Amberly!" said Orla sternly.

Anger and sadness were written all over Amberly's face and her mother softened for a moment as she sighed. "Amberly...It's only because I love you!" Orla said as she grabbed Amberly's arm.

"Leave me alone!" Amberly said as she pulled away from her mother's grip and ran and leapt to her room. Safflower followed behind her. Her tiny wings could barely keep up with Amberly's speed and before she made it to Amberly's room, Amberly had already entered it and slammed her bedroom door shut.

"Amberly! Amberly! Let me in!" shouted Safflower as she knocked on Amberly's door with her tiny, long appendages. Amberly suddenly opened her door with an angry look in her eyes and Safflower flew inside Amberly's bedroom.

"Are you ok?" Safflower asked worriedly.

"I don't want to talk about it," Amberly said as she slammed her bedroom door shut. She leapt onto her bed and lay down on her stomach. She stared at her father's portrait, which she had placed back on her nightstand, while Safflower sat quietly at the foot of her bed.

"What am I going to do, Safflower?" Amberly said solemnly as she continued to stare at her father's portrait.

Safflower flew above Amberly and gently landed on Amberly's back. "I think you should just get some rest now," she said.

"I don't want to rest. I have to think," said Amberly.

Safflower flew over to Amberly's pillow and laid her little butterfly body down. "Ok. You think. I'll rest," Safflower said with a yawn as she closed her weary eyes. The warmth of Amberly's pillow and the cool breeze blowing in through Amberly's tiny cracked window lulled Safflower to sleep.

Hours passed and the long afternoon melted into sundown. Meanwhile, Amberly had been tossing and turning in her bed. She was trying to think of a plan that would convince her mother that she was perfectly capable of taking sword fighting lessons. Since she was so strong, Amberly felt that holding a sword with one hand would be a snap.

As her body relaxed, she finally began to feel the weight of her eyelids. The moonlight lit up her room and Amberly took one last glance at her father's portrait before falling into a deep sleep.

Chapter Eight

The morning sun crept into Amberly's little room and Safflower was wide awake. Amberly was still fast asleep when Safflower flew over to the nightstand and picked up her little mug made of twine. She made sure Amberly was still sleeping soundly and then she flew out of the window quietly. She didn't realize that Amberly had woken up and was watching her fly out of the window.

Amberly knew what Safflower was up to and she smirked as she sat up in her bed. She shoved her two pillows beneath the multicolored, quilted blanket that her mother had made her, and she made the lumpy pillows look like she was sleeping beneath the blanket.

Safflower flew back in through the window with her mug full of icy dew drops. She hovered over Amberly's bed while she held her mug between her front appendages. "Rise and shine sunshine!" she shouted. With her back appendages, she pulled down the blanket covering the lump on Amberly's bed, revealing the two pillows instead of Amberly.

"Hey!" Safflower shouted.

Amberly suddenly popped out from under the bed and let out a loud roar, causing Safflower to scream and drop her mug filled with icy dew drops right onto the floor. "Aaah!" she shouted. "You scared me half to death!"

Amberly tried to hold in her laughter but failed miserably. "I'm sorry, Saffy…But, you should have seen your face!" She picked up

Safflower's mug off the floor and then crawled back into her bed with the now-empty mug still in her hand.

Safflower fluttered down and landed on the bed beside Amberly.

"It's fairy rest day, Safflower. Why are we up so early?" asked Amberly.

"I was thinking it would be a good day for you to help the animals," said Safflower, who fluttered over Amberly and gently landed on her stomach. "We can search for those who are caught in those awful traps the mortals have been hiding."

Amberly nodded. Safflower could tell that Amberly was lost in thought as she glided her hand over the clay mug that Safflower had decorated with woven twine, and then admired Safflower's wings. "Whatcha thinking about?" Safflower asked.

Amberly looked at the tiny mug again. "Safflower, could you teach me how to weave twine like this?"

"Of course!" said Safflower proudly.

"Wait here!" Amberly said with excitement as she jumped out of her bed and grabbed her running stick from behind her nightstand. She was moving so fast she didn't realize that Safflower had switched resting spots. Safflower had been sitting on part of Amberly's nightgown and she was almost tossed right off the bed as Amberly jumped up.

"Sorry, Safflower!" said Amberly as she leapt out of her room using her running stick.

Safflower sighed, sat on Amberly's bed, and waited patiently for her to come back. She was extremely curious to know what Amberly was planning, and whatever her plan was, she hoped to be a part of it.

A few minutes passed, and Amberly finally rushed back into her room with spools of orange and red thread that she had borrowed from her mother's sewing basket. She plopped herself back down on her bed and studied Safflower's mug once again.

"Whatcha doin?" Safflower asked curiously. Amberly looked at Safflower with an intense stare. Safflower could tell she had something on her mind.

"I have an idea. And if it works, I'll have my balance back and I won't need my stupid running stick anymore!" said Amberly.

"So, what's the plan?" Safflower asked.

Amberly was so involved in her thoughts that she didn't respond right away, and she quickly tossed the spools of thread into her brown satchel bag. "I'll tell you when we get to the forest, Safflower."

"Yippee! I love the forest on fairy rest day. No pixie pollination training!" Safflower shouted happily as she flew over to Amberly's little blue closet and assisted Amberly with her wardrobe. As she helped Amberly put on her amber-colored arm bracers and the rest of her fairy warrior outfit, Safflower's mind wandered. She was looking forward to whatever Amberly was planning because having a plan was good. Plans made Amberly happy, and that's all that Safflower wanted—for Amberly to be happy.

"What are you doing, Amberly?" she asked as Amberly removed her sword from her closet.

"Don't worry about it, Safflower. Trust me," Amberly said as she slid her sword into her scabbard and strapped it to her back.

"But, if your mother sees you with that sword, Amberly…"

"She won't!" Amberly interrupted. "You worry too much." She grabbed her running stick and put her father's portrait back in her satchel bag. "Lets' go!"

"Ok…" said Safflower as she jumped on Amberly's shoulder.

Amberly slowly opened her bedroom door and looked to her right and then to her left down the little hallway. "Don't say a word," she whispered.

Safflower looked at Amberly and nodded.

In one swift leap, Amberly quietly moved through the hallway. Her mother and sister were still sleeping in their beds, which gave her the chance to quietly run out of the cottage's front door with Safflower on her shoulder.

Chapter Nine

The forest was still and peaceful now as Amberly and Safflower made their way to their favorite sparkling pond, which lay just above an old grassy hill blanketed with brightly-colored wildflowers every spring. Amberly loved springtime. The forest was enchanted with bright-purple, gold, pink, lavender, and blue wildflowers. Their bright colors were reflected in the still, glassy pond where Amberly and Safflower stopped to drink the fresh cool water.

Amberly knelt on a small stone at the edge of the pond, scooped up a handful of cold, clear, water and took a sip. She hadn't even realized how thirsty she was. Looking up at the sky, she made a long wish to the heavens that she might be reunited with her father soon. She looked at her reflection in the small pond and splashed the luxuriously cool water on to her face, while Safflower flew swiftly above the water's surface.

Amberly loved watching Safflower fly and Safflower loved having Amberly's captivated attention. When she noticed Amberly's smiling eyes fixated on her, she fluttered her little butterfly fairy wings as fast as she could, flying high above the pond and then down toward the water with great speed.

She skimmed the pond's surface and flew right over two dragonflies that had no idea what was coming. Amberly laughed hysterically and placed her hand on her own impish, paralyzed little wing as she watched Safflower fly so effortlessly.

As Amberly sat at the edge of the pond, she slowly pulled out the spools of red and orange thread she had borrowed from her mother's sewing supply and gazed at the willow tree standing a few feet away from her. The dried twigs at the base of the willow's trunk caught her attention. Lost in thought, she quickly jumped to her feet and with the help of her running stick, ran and leapt toward the willow tree. Once she arrived at the tree, she picked up two long, dry twigs from the ground.

Safflower was busy racing a dragonfly across the pond. When she noticed Amberly gathering the twigs, she stopped and quickly flew over to Amberly, who was under the willow tree.

"Hey, what are those for?" Safflower asked curiously as she landed on Amberly's shoulder and pointed to the twigs.

"We need to soak them," said Amberly.

"Ok. Whatever you say," Safflower said as she held on to Amberly's shoulder. With a start, Amberly ran and leapt toward the edge of the pond carrying her two long twigs in her right hand. Once she reached the end of the pond, she kneeled at the water's edge and held the twigs under water.

"I don't know what you're up to, Amberly, but I hope it's not going to get you into trouble."

"Oh, Safflower. You worry too much," Amberly replied calmly as she continued to soak the long twigs.

After a few minutes of having held the twigs under water, Amberly pulled them out and set the drenched twigs on the ground beside her. She smiled when she saw how pliable the branches were and she began to shape each branch in the form of a tear drop. "Safflower, can you please fetch my satchel for me?" she said, as she pointed toward the willow tree.

"Sure," Safflower said, and she flew to the tree and grabbled Amberly's satchel that was still resting in the willow's shade.

"Thank you!" Amberly said with a smile as Safflower set the satchel down beside her.

Safflower had no idea what Amberly was up to, but whatever it was, it seemed to be making Amberly very happy, and that was all Safflower wanted—for Amberly happy.

Amberly laid the teardrop-shaped twigs on the ground. The sound of the pond's water rippling in the wind seemed to relax her as the sun shined down on her. She pulled her sword out of the scabbard on her back, and with one swift motion cut long pieces of red and orange thread. Then she picked up the first teardrop-shaped twig and tied the two ends of the twig together, so that it would hold its shape.

"Here, help me," Amberly said. She held out a few strands of thread in front of Safflower, who was fluttering above her head. Safflower snatched the strands of thread from Amberly's hand and flew over to the other tear-shaped twig on the ground. She tied the two ends of the second twig together, which formed another oblong, teardrop-shaped twig.

Amberly then arranged the two teardrop twigs one above the other on the ground and with Safflower's help, tied both teardrop-shaped twigs together, arranging them in what looked like the perfect shape of a fairy wing.

"Safflower, since you know how to weave, do you think you could create a spider web with this thread inside of my twig-framed fairy wing?" Amberly asked as she held out the two spools of red and orange thread.

Safflower looked at the wing-shaped twigs lying on the grass, still wet with pond water. "Hmm…I might be able to," she said, as she scratched her head with her front appendage.

"Here," said Amberly. She tossed a spool of orange thread to Safflower, who caught it midair.

Eagerly, Safflower began to loosely wrap the thread around the top twig, which created a row of loops that hung down inside the top part of the wing shape. She stared at the first layer of threaded loops for a moment, and then began to weave the spool of thread in and out of each of the first layer of loops inside of the makeshift wing.

This created a second layer of loops. Safflower continued to do this until she filled the entire twig wing frame with what looked like a spider web made of thread.

Next, Safflower picked up the spool of red thread and wove a few more rows of loops in the middle of the teardrop-shaped twig. She managed to do the same thing with the attached, bottom portion of the wing.

To Amberly's surprise, Safflower had made a beautiful red and orange netting inside of what looked like a fairy wing made of twigs and thread!

Amberly was beside herself with joy. She let out a loud gasp and shrieked with excitement. "Oh Safflower! It's perfect!" she shouted. After Safflower had tied the last loop securely to the damp, twig-framed wing, Amberly quickly cut the red thread from the spool with her sword. "Safflower! It's beautiful! Come here. Help me tie my new wing brace to my scabbard."

Safflower caught two long pieces of orange thread that Amberly tossed to her and tied one end of the thread to the bottom of the twig wing brace. She tied the second strand of orange thread to the top of the wing brace. Next, in order to support Amberly's left, paralyzed wing, she tied the two free ends of the thread to Amberly's scabbard strap behind Amberly's left shoulder.

Safflower smiled with a twinkle in her eye. She stared at Amberly, who was standing proudly, sporting her new wing brace.

Amberly began to walk along the edge of the pond. "Safflower, look at me! I'm not even wobbling! I don't even need my running stick!" she shouted at the top of her lungs.

Safflower let out a joyful laugh. "Woohoo! You look amazing, Amberly!"

Amberly spun in a circle on her feet then leapt in the air and landed perfectly upright without losing her balance. "Now for the real test," she said.

Safflower held her breath. If she'd had fingers, she would have crossed them because she knew just what Amberly was about to do.

"Wish me luck, Safflower," said Amberly.

"Good luck! Now, off you go!" said Safflower excitedly.

Amberly quickly faced forward and began to run through the forest. She laughed the entire time as she ran and leapt through the air without the help of her running stick. She even landed perfectly on her own two feet without falling over!

"I did it!" Amberly shouted as she laughed hysterically. "It's working, Safflower!" It's working!"

"Woohoo! Yippee!" Safflower shouted as she flew behind Amberly, who was running and leaping about.

Amberly landed on her two feet once again without toppling over and she let out a victorious scream. "Come on Safflower!" she said as she held out her hand and waited for Safflower to land on it. Then she carefully placed Safflower onto her shoulder.

"You did it, Amberly! You did it! You've kept your balance without using your running stick!"

Amberly smiled and let out a sigh of relief as she slowly sat down beside the pond. She had run and leapt around the pond three times without losing her balance one bit. "Do you know what this means, Safflower?"

"Umm…That you don't need your running stick, anymore?"

"Yes. And??"

"And you won't need your acorn helmet anymore?"

"Besides that."

"Uh…"

"I can take sword fighting lessons, now!"

Safflower blinked her eyes and stared at Amberly in shock. "Oh, um, well…we should see what your mother says about it first, Amberly."

Amberly shook her head and adjusted her new wing brace to make sure it was secured tightly to the scabbard strap behind her shoulder.

"Amberly…what are you up to?" Safflower asked nervously. Amberly had that look in her eye that Safflower knew all too well. It was the look she got right before she was about to do something that she shouldn't. "Amberly?"

"Hang on, Safflower. We're going to pay Uncle Orin a visit." Like a flash of lightning, Amberly was off and running. She ran as fast as she could, leapt high into the air every so often, and landed perfectly upright on her own two feet. She just couldn't wait to show her Uncle Orin her new wing brace. Once he saw that she was able to balance without using her running stick to hold her up, she was sure he would teach her everything he knew about sword fighting.

Chapter Ten

Beautiful wildflowers and honeysuckle lined Orin's walkway. Once Amberly and Safflower finally reached the tiny cottage's door, Amberly knocked firmly. Her Uncle Orin was hard of hearing, so she called out to him as loudly as she could. "Uncle! We're here!" Amberly yelled as Safflower peered into Orin's front window.

"Orin! Orin! Here he comes! Here he comes!" said Safflower excitedly. Safflower loved Uncle Orin with all her heart. Orin had rescued Safflower from a horrible rainstorm when she was just a newly hatched fairy butterfly. It wasn't until Safflower matured and grew older, when Orin asked her to be Amberly's watcher. He thought that this way, Amberly would always have someone looking out for her and she would never be alone. Not that being alone is always a bad thing, but at any rate, Orin wanted Amberly to always have someone watching over her, given that she was born with a paralyzed wing. Safflower was so excited to see Orin that she decided it would be fun to surprise him, so she hid beneath Amberly's hair.

Orin's cottage door suddenly opened. There he stood with a crabby frown, which suddenly morphed into a gigantic smile. "Amberly!" he said with a happy laugh. Amberly rushed into his arms. His embrace was so warm that it filled Amberly's heart with joy.

"What? What is this?" Orin said as he gently touched Amberly's twig wing brace. Amberly smiled excitedly. "It's my new wing, Uncle Orin!"

"Well, well, well. You've finally done it, haven't you? You've figured out a way!" said Orin with a laugh.

"And I've brought my sword! I don't need my running stick anymore. I can take sword fighting lessons now, Uncle Orin!"

Orin's face lit up and he let out a loud chuckle. "Amberly, that's wonderful! And your mother? She's ok with you learning to handle your sword now?"

"Well, yes. She said whenever my balance was corrected, then it would be ok. So, here I am!" Amberly said forcefully.

"Come in! Come in!" he said with youthful enthusiasm.

Safflower suddenly popped out from beneath Amberly's hair and soared around Orin excitedly. "Surprise! Did ya forget about me?" she giggled.

"Safflower! How could I ever forget about you!" Orin held out his hand and laughed as Safflower landed on his palm. "Come in, dear ones!" he said as he turned and walked inside. Amberly followed behind them.

Uncle Orin's living room was packed to the brim with old sorcery books. Every little end table; his old, tattered, brown sofa; the fluffy beige chairs; and a wooden table were all covered with beautifully bound books. The book covers were bright and reflective of every fairy wing color in existence. As Amberly followed her Uncle Orin through this little, dimly-lit living room filled with oak tree furniture, she noticed his grey hair had gotten longer and a little stragglier since she had last seen him a few weeks prior. But his wings were still a gorgeous, mothy white and his eyes, a piercing blue, and they practically glowed in the candlelit room.

The three finally entered Orin's study, his sacred haven that was filled with his collections of swords and books. Brightly-colored landscape paintings lined the walls and portraits of Amberly's fairy ancestors were hung with pride. Some of them had been actual fairy warriors themselves. Amberly admired the ancient fairy faces of generations past. She wondered what the earth had been like during her fairy ancestors' long lifetimes. Whimsical fairies usually lived about 400 years and it was amazing to think about all of the sunrises and sunsets her ancestors had seen. Uncle Orin was 300 years old and he was still amazingly fit for his fairy age. The lean muscles in his arms made his fairy body appear to be somewhat younger than he was despite his long grey hair.

As Amberly's eyes drifted to the corner of the room, she noticed Uncle Orin's sword leaning against the old bookshelf and she stared at its shiny blade.

"Come now young one. Let's start with your stance, shall we?" he said.

"Sure," said Amberly as she walked to the middle of the room and met him face to face. Safflower perched herself right on Orin's desk and watched them curiously. She looked so small in comparison to all of Uncle Orin's unraveled paper scrolls, which were scattered on his desk. Her wings fluttered slowly as she looked on. Safflower made for a wonderful captive audience.

Uncle Orin stared at Amberly wide eyed.

She knew that was her cue to prepare for the lesson he was about to divulge.

"Now, I want you to imagine your opponent, Amberly. In your mind, who do you see?"

Well, that's easy, Amberly said to herself. "I see a Nyxie fairy from the Dark Forest," she grumbled.

Orin smiled at Amberly proudly. "Ah ha! So, you've been keeping up with your reading, I presume?"

Centuries ago it was said that the Dark Forest had always been separated from Whimsical Land by a magic portal. Where this magical portal lay was unknown to the Whimsical fairies.

Uncle Orin was the last of the aged fairies to believe that the Dark Forest and its magical portal existed. As legend had it, 2000 years ago, there were five Whimsical fairy couples that unfortunately, had been cursed with lovers' quarrels. The bride fairies had been abandoned by the groom fairies just before they were about to be wed on Fairy Wedding Day. It was said that the heartbroken female fairies were devastated and filled with great sorrow. They eventually ran deep into the forest and were never seen again.

According to the legend, the Nyxie fairies from the Dark Forest were drawn to the Whimsical fairies whenever a moment of sadness weakened their fairy hearts. When the Whimsical fairies' hearts weakened, the Nyxies were able to magically steal their energy and the colorful magic pixie dust that permeated the Whimsical fairies' wings.

After having been stripped of their wings' colorful, magic pixie dust, the poor heartbroken, female Whimsical fairies of the past turned grey and became trapped in the Dark Forest, never to be seen again. The portal that they had fallen through was never found again.

According to the book, *The Secret of the Fairy Warriors,* the Whimsical fairies' hopelessness is what reopened the portal to the Dark Forest. Amberly believed her father, who had been filled with sadness the moment he realized Amberly could not fly, had fallen through the dark forest's portal when she was two years old. Her Uncle Orin believed this to be true as well. That is why he'd agreed to train Amberly to become a fairy warrior. Amberly knew that one day, she and her Uncle Orin were going to find this portal together. And, once they found this portal, they would enter the Dark Forest and find her father and her distant cousin, Nissa, who had been stolen from Whimsical Land as well.

"Amberly! Stay focused!" Uncle Orin cried out.

Amberly nodded her head and focused on the moment at hand.

"Now that you have your opponent, imagine a mirror of yourself. Remember, your toes should be pointed at your opponent," said Orin authoritatively.

Amberly smiled at her dear uncle and then quickly switched on her serious, studious, expression. She pointed her right foot forward just like her Uncle Orin had told her to do and pointed her toes right at him.

"Good. Your back foot need not point at your opponent. You should be able to bend your knees and squat easily," said Orin.

Amberly squatted her knees then resumed her upright position.

Orin rushed to her aid and placed his hand on her back. "Don't hunch your back. Keep it straight," he said.

"Oh. Right," Amberly said as she stood up straight.

"Your hips and shoulders should be in tandem with each other when you move them. Now, move your sword into fighting stance and hold it out in front. Your arm should be just below shoulder height."

"Ok. Got it," Amberly said attentively.

Uncle Orin stood directly in front of her with his sword in fighting position. "Put your sword out in front of you like this," he said as he extended his sword forward.

Amberly moved her arm forward with her sword's blade pointing straight up.

"Your arm should be just below shoulder height. Elbow slightly bent. Hold the sword fairly high."

"Like this?" Amberly said as she held her arm out, not letting her forearm rise above her shoulder.

"Good. Your guard is high and it's out," Uncle Orin said as he held his sword out and away from him. "Why do you think your sword should be held this way, Amberly?"

Amberly just stared at her uncle for a moment. Her sword was facing outward, close to her uncle's face now.

"Well, the closer my blade is to my opponent, the easier it is to attack them."

"You mean stab them!" Uncle Orin said sternly.

Amberly flinched the moment Uncle Orin raised his voice. "Yes... stab them," she replied after clearing her throat.

"The Nyxie fairies are dangerous beings, Amberly. And you have to be quick enough to stab them before they can conjure up their black magic!" Orin moved his sword in a figure-eight motion in front of Amberly's face.

Amberly didn't bat an eye. She was utterly lost in a trance and captivated by the swift moves her Uncle Orin made with his sword, until she felt a sudden flutter of satiny soft wings on her cheek. "Safflower!" Amberly said with a startled yell.

"It's almost dinner time! You know your mother will worry, Amberly!" Uncle Orin gave Safflower a curious stare.

Amberly finally came out of her concentration mode and a sudden sinking feeling filled her gut.

Orin looked at Amberly wide eyed and startled.

"Oh, where did the day go! I'm sorry, Uncle Orin, I must go. We will be back next week for my next lesson, though!" said Amberly as she rushed forward to give her Uncle Orin a kiss on the cheek.

With that, Amberly ran out of the study with Safflower hanging on to her shoulder. Amberly could hear Uncle Orin fluttering his wings behind her. He barely kept up with Amberly's pace and she didn't look back until she exited the front door.

"Bye Uncle Orin!" she said loudly as she waved goodbye.

"Don't forget to work on your stance!"

"I won't!" Amberly shouted as she ran along the cobblestone pathway and disappeared into the forest.

Chapter Eleven

Amberly could smell her mother's delicious biscuits baking as she ran up the little walkway to her family's cottage. She was so excited to show her mother the new wing brace that she and Safflower had made that she could hardly contain herself.

Just as she turned the knob on her fairy cottage's door, Calista opened the door at the same time.

"Amberly! Where've you been?" Calista asked with concern. "We were so worried about you!"

"Hi, sis! What do you think?" Amberly said as she wiggled her left shoulder, bringing attention to her new wing brace. Her sword was tucked snug in her belt behind her, hiding it from her sister's view.

The bottom portion of her running stick was lodged inside her scabbard on her back. It looked quite strange since the top off it towered high above the back of Amberly's head at a slight slant.

"What? How? Oh Amberly! This is amazing!" Calista shouted as she hugged Amberly. "I'm sorry I got so angry with you at Fairy Wedding rehearsal," she said lovingly. "I've just been feeling so stressed out about this whole wedding thing."

Relieved that her sister was no longer angry at her, Amberly smiled and shrugged. "It's ok. Don't worry, the wedding will be beautiful! I'm just sorry I'm a horrible dancer."

Calista laughed with her little sister. "It's not your fault, sis. Mother! Come look at Amberly!" she shouted while Safflower flew above them with excitement.

Orla flew into the living room as she wiped her hands on her little apron. She landed near the sofa and gasped when she saw Amberly standing straight and giggling with Calista. "Amberly? What's this?" Orla said with a smile as she touched Amberly's wing brace.

"I can keep my balance now, Mother!"

"How on earth did you come up with this? It's beautiful!" said Orla. "You're keeping your balance perfectly!"

"Yep. I don't even need this anymore!" Amberly said as she quickly pulled her running stick out of her scabbard on her back and tossed it onto the sofa. Unfortunately, her sword fell out of her belt's grip and fell to the floor with a loud clink.

Amberly froze for a moment and Safflower floated down slowly onto her shoulder. They stared nervously at Orla, whose smile quickly faded. Calista looked at her mother then at Amberly with concern.

"Amberly..." Orla's voice was low and monotone. It was the kind of voice she used right before she was about to give a scolding.

Amberly slowly bent down and picked up her sword. "Just let me explain, Mother," she said as she quickly slid her sword into the scabbard on her back.

"Amberly!! What are you doing with that sword! I specifically told you to never remove that sword from your closet!" shouted Orla.

Amberly took a deep breath before she spoke. "I know, Mother, I'm sorry. But you said I can take sword fighting lessons once I could keep my balance, and look! I can keep my balance perfectly now with my wing brace!" She ran around the living room, did a summersault over the little wooden coffee table in the middle of the room, and then landed on her feet right next to Calista, who laughed hysterically as she fluttered her gorgeous wings.

"Well, she does have a point, Mother." said Calista with a smile. She hugged her little sister. "Oh, Amberly I'm so happy for you!"

"Thanks big sis!" said Amberly with a triumphant smile.

Orla moved closer to Amberly and held her little fairy daughter's face in her hands. "Listen to me. I'm so happy that you can balance yourself with your new wing brace, sweetheart, I really am. But, you don't even know how to handle a sword, which is why I told you to never remove it from your closet."

Amberly backed up a little and pulled her scimitar sword from her scabbard. "Umm, well, I learned a lot today. Look! I know the proper way to hold my sword now!"

Orla flinched. "What do you mean, you learned already, Amberly?"

Amberly's smile faded and she slowly put the sword back in her scabbard. "Mother, ok…sit down and I'll explain."

"I don't want to sit down," said Orla.

Calista looked at her mother and then back at Amberly again. "How about we all sit down at the dinner table, Mother, and let Amberly explain while we eat?" she said in a soothing voice.

"Oh, yes. Please! I'm starving!" Amberly said as she started to walk toward the kitchen with Calista and her mother floating and fluttering behind her.

The three took their seats at the beautifully set kitchen table. Hot soup, bread, salad, berry pie and a bowl of nectar for Safflower had already been placed neatly on the table.

"This looks delicious!" said Amberly as her mother began to serve the salad.

"Ok. Now, what is it you want to tell me, Amberly?" said Orla sternly.

"That wing brace is amazing! How did you make it?" Calista asked.

Amberly smiled as she gulped a bite of food down. "Well, first we soaked a couple of twigs that had fallen from a willow tree."

"Amberly," her mother interrupted.

Amberly took a sip of water from her wooden cup then began to speak softly and hesitantly. "Uncle Orin gave me a sword fighting lesson today."

Orla's fork suddenly dropped onto her plate and she let out a loud gasp while her eyes focused intently on Amberly and Calista. "What?!" she shouted.

Calista put her hand on her mother's arm, trying desperately to calm her.

"Amberly, how dare you go off and take sword fighting lessons behind my back!"

Amberly flinched. She had never seen her mother look so angry before. "But, you said I could if my balance was corrected!"

Orla suddenly leaned back in her chair. "What am I going to do with you, Amberly?"

Feeling the immense tension in the room, Calista chimed in. "Mother, why don't we just listen to what Amberly has to say?"

Amberly glanced at Calista and then back at her mother's angry face. "I didn't mean to take sword fighting lessons behind your back, Mother, but..."

"But what, Amberly?" Orla shouted.

"We were already halfway to Uncle Orin's house after I made my wing brace and I don't know…I just was so happy that I could balance myself, I couldn't wait to show Uncle Orin."

Orla closed her eyes and shook her head. "You disobeyed me. You deliberately left our cottage with that dangerous weapon in your hand, Amberly!"

Amberly looked down at her plate ashamedly and then managed to look up at her mother again. "But I had it safe in my scabbard, Mother. I wasn't in any danger."

Orla dug her fork into her salad aggressively and took a quick bite and a long sip of water before she spoke again. "Well, I'm afraid you won't be leaving this cottage on Fairy Rest Day for a long while now."

"What?" shouted Amberly.

"Mother, don't you think that's a little harsh?" said Calista with concern.

"Stay out of this, Calista!" Orla shouted. "Amberly, you are not

68

to leave this cottage for three months except for fairy pollination training and Fairy Wedding Day dance rehearsals.

"Three months? That's too long! Mother, in three months I'll be a fairy warrior if I continue my lessons with Uncle Orin!"

Orla started to spread butter angrily on a biscuit. "Three months. My decision is final, Amberly."

With tears in her eyes, Calista looked at her mother and then at her little sister. She wished she could say something to help her little fairy sister out but she knew that nothing she could say at this point would change her mother's mind.

"But, don't you want me to rescue Father?" asked Amberly.

"Amberly! That's enough! Just stop with this obsession you have!"

"No! No, I won't stop! Please Mother, let me take sword fighting lessons! You won't regret it, I promise!"

Orla suddenly got to her feet and stretched out her hand. "Give me your sword."

"What?" Amberly said in shock.

"Give me your sword, Amberly. It's for your own good," said Orla.

"No!" Amberly cried.

Orla's eyes suddenly turned red. She was fuming with anger as she flew to Amberly's side. Amberly quickly stood up and moved away from her mother.

Safflower became extremely anxious and landed on Amberly's shoulder. "Amberly, why don't we go to your room and relax a bit, yes? Just give your mother the sword," she whispered.

Amberly couldn't believe what Safflower had just said to her. And she couldn't believe that her mother was actually trying to take away her sword! "No, Safflower! What are you saying?"

"Give it to me, Amberly!" Orla shouted. She tried to pull Amberly's sword from her scabbard, but Amberly pushed her mother's hand away.

"No! Mother, how could you?" Amberly said with tears in her eyes.

"Amberly, I'm giving you until three to hand over that sword. One…two…"

"No! Never!" Amberly shouted. With that, she spun around and accidently knocked over her chair. Then she ran out of the kitchen through the living room and out of the fairy cottage's front door.

"Amberly! Wait!" Calista shouted as she flew after her sister, but Amberly was too fast and she was already gone. "Amberly!" Calista shouted again as Orla flew up behind her and began to cry.

"What am I going to do with that sister of yours, Calista?" Orla said in between sobs.

"I think you've done enough, Mother."

"I am just looking out for her, Calista! You'll understand one day when you're a mother!"

"Can we just finish dinner?" said Calista.

Orla nodded her head, wiped her eyes, and followed Calista back to the kitchen table.

"Don't worry, Mother, the sun will be going down soon, so she'll be back. You know how much she hates the dark."

Chapter Twelve

Amberly ran so fast through the forest that the trees looked like green blobs as she raced by them with lightning speed. The flowers, deer, rabbits, and shrubs all blended together in one amazingly fast flying mass as Amberly whooshed past them. Avery and Spice happened to be flying in the forest when they saw Amberly rush by. She could vaguely hear Avery calling out her name behind her.

"Amberly! Come back!" Avery yelled.

But Amberly was at least a mile away by now and she could barely hear Avery and Spice calling her name. She couldn't stop running even if she tried. Her legs continued to run while tears streamed down her cheeks. The cold wind felt like tiny swords stabbing her face. She wouldn't have stopped running if it weren't for a pebble that suddenly appeared right in her path. It caused her to trip and fall forward into a patch of cool green moss that was taking over the area below a large weeping willow tree.

Amberly let out a loud cry as she landed in a pool of cold mud between the willow tree's exposed roots. She desperately tried to gain her composure after the fall, but it was no use. Her cries were loud, and tears ran freely down her face. She crawled close to the willow's trunk and leaned her head onto its thick bark.

As Amberly sat with her little body flinching with every cry, she was suddenly startled by Safflower, who fluttered her wings against Amberly's cheek as she sat on Amberly's shoulder.

"Amberly! Amberly, it's ok!" said Safflower.

Amberly cupped her tiny butterfly fairy in her hand and held Safflower close to her chest while letting out a soft cry. Safflower sadly burrowed her little head into Amberly's chest and her comforting little presence finally slowed Amberly's hysterical cries. Amberly knew Avery and Spice would probably catch up with her soon, so, she wiped the tears from her cheeks and tried to calm herself down.

Amberly took a deep breath and looked up. Avery and Spice were flying toward her with the whimsies, Bliss and Remi riding on their backs. The little whimsies looked so adorable riding on her dear friends' backs that Amberly would have smiled if it weren't for the tears rolling off her cheeks and onto the soft patch of ground she sat on.

Just as Amberly's tears hit the ground, the earth beneath her began to shake. It shook so hard that the ground broke open! Safflower held on onto Amberly's scabbard strap and the two were scared stiff. Amberly was paralyzed with fear as she watched a large crack in the earth travel right to where she was sitting. Before she knew it, her legs and waist were sinking into a large black hole.

Amberly held on to the edge of the ground with all her might while her legs dangled inside the black hole. She quickly pulled her legs out of the black void in the ground and climbed up the oak tree behind her. As she stared down at the large, gaping hole in the ground, her mind began to race. "Safflower, this has to be the portal to the Dark Forest! This may be the only way to save my father! What should we do?" The earth rumbled below her as she sat on the oak tree's branch while looking down.

"I-I don't know, Amberly... But I'm with you no matter what you decide!" shouted Safflower.

As Amberly stared down at the gaping hole in the ground, she took a deep breath. "Hold on, Safflower!" she shouted just as Avery and Spice ran toward the oak tree. They gasped and shuddered when the saw the black hole in front of the tree.

"Amberly! Jump down! I'll catch you!" Avery screamed.

But Amberly didn't hear Avery because the ground was shaking and rumbling so loudly. With one swift move, she jumped off the tree branch and let herself fall right into the black, open trench in the ground.

Safflower screamed as she held tightly onto Amberly's scabbard strap and nuzzled close to Amberly's neck. She and Amberly were almost consumed by the black hole just as Avery, Spice, and the little whimsies finally caught up to her. "Amberly!" Spice shouted.

"Amberly! Amberly!" Bliss and Corliss shouted out in unison, but it was too late. Amberly fell straight through the open trench in the ground and in a flash she and Safflower were gone.

Chapter Thirteen

Amberly and Safflower were falling so fast underground that they could barely catch their breath. Little Safflower screamed hysterically with her tiny little voice while Amberly held her close to her chest and was careful not to crush her tiny wings.

The two fell so fast down the black trench that Amberly's body felt as though it were going into shock from the drastic temperature change. It was so dark that she could barely see anything at all except for a few tree roots that whirled passed her as she spiraled down into what seemed like a long hollow tunnel. Holding Safflower close, Amberly let out a loud scream as she was suddenly forced sideways and then upwards by a strong, inexplicable force of wind of some sort.

Without any warning, Amberly and Safflower shot straight up toward the earth's surface. Amberly felt the coolness of wet soil along with a prickly sensation of tree roots scratching her face as her head suddenly broke through wet soil. As Amberly's head popped up through the earth, an unseen force pushed the rest of her body upward through the wet ground and she landed on her feet. She quickly placed Safflower on her shoulder and Safflower nuzzled close.

While Amberly stood on unfamiliar ground, the first thing she and Safflower noticed was how cold and dark the world had suddenly become. It even smelled different—like wet dirt. The black sky was lit by moonlight and a million twinkling stars.

Amberly looked around slowly at her surroundings. In the

moonlight, the trees and shrubs looked like black shadows and the grass looked somewhat like shiny black licorice.

Safflower looked up at Amberly sadly. "Where...where are we, Amberly?"

Amberly looked down at her little watcher. "We're definitely not in Whimsical Land anymore, that's for sure."

"Is this the Dark Forest?" Safflower asked as she looked at Amberly with fright. Her bright eyes were consumed by fear and sadness and her little body fell limp with defeat on Amberly's shoulder. She'd never really thought they would find the Dark Forest, and now that they were there, she really wished they could go back to Whimsical Land.

Amberly continued to look around the strange land. There were no flowers at all and not a drop of color in sight. The moon was so big and bright that it looked as if one could touch it.

Amberly's attention was suddenly directed to an odd sound. It sounded like someone weeping close by. "Safflower, do you hear that?"

Safflower perked up and without warning flew in the direction of the crying. Safflower hated when anyone cried.

Amberly ran after her. "Safflower, wait! Come back!"

Safflower flew around an old, dark, evergreen tree with black leaves and disappeared behind its thick trunk. Amberly ran toward the tree as fast as she could. She came to an abrupt halt and stopped right in front of a tiny fairy with shimmery purple hair, velvety, purple wings, and blue eyes. The strange, yet pretty, fairy had a chalky-white complexion and wore a dress made of purple satin. She was the saddest little fairy Amberly had ever laid eyes on. Every time the little fairy let out a pathetic whimper while she held her own head in her hands, Amberly cringed

The purple-haired fairy was unaware of Safflower hovering above her head with concern.

Amberly shuddered at the sight of Safflower flying near this stranger fairy. She wasn't sure if this strange little fairy could be trusted. They were in the Dark Forest, for goodness sake! Uncle Orin had always warned Amberly of the dangers of the Dark Forest. So many Whimsical fairies had been trapped here, according to the legends, and Amberly truly believed her father and cousin were among them.

"Safflower, come here!" Amberly said sternly in a loud whisper. Just then, the purple-haired fairy stopped crying and looked right at Amberly.

The strange little fairy let out a loud scream and jumped to her feet. "Who...who are you?"

In a mad rush, Safflower flew toward Amberly and landed on her shoulder.

"I'm Amberly. Who are you?"

"Onyx," the little fairy said as she shielded her eyes with her hands, trying to block the bright, reddish-orange hue that seemed to generate off Amberly's wings. The brightness was almost too much for Onyx's eyes to bear. "Why do you look like that?" she asked, nervously.

"Look like what?" said Amberly.

"So...so bright!" said Onyx.

Amberly slowly walked backward and suddenly had the strong urge to run. She had no idea what was going to happen to her in this strange land, and where there was one Nyxie fairy, surely there would have to be more. Even though Onyx didn't outwardly seem like a threat, Amberly thought there would be others who would not take so kindly to a foreign fairy that looked so drastically different from them. That was the unfortunate nature of all forest creatures, so why would fairies be any different?

As she stared at Onyx's shocked face, Amberly started to back up even faster. She was just about to sprint away when Onyx suddenly cried out.

"Wait! Don't go! I think I know who you are now!"

Something about Onyx's intensity made Amberly reluctantly stop in her tracks.

Onyx suddenly sported a huge smile. "You must be the one I've been waiting for! The angel my grandfather predicted!"

Amberly shook her head and stared at the little fairy, who called herself Onyx. "I'm not an angel. You must be mistaken."

"Well, whatever you are, my grandfather said you would be here by this very willow and here you are. I just wasn't expecting a fairy that looked like you!" Onyx said as she moved closer to Amberly.

"What's wrong with a fairy that looks like me?" Amberly said defensively as she stared at the beautiful, shiny, black gemstone on a gold chain that Onyx wore around her neck. It had to be the most beautiful piece of jewelry Amberly had ever seen.

"Oh, I didn't mean to sound rude. I just..." Onyx was suddenly interrupted by an odd sound that escaped her little satchel bag. The bag was made of the silkiest black raven feathers Amberly had ever seen.

Bleep bleep. There was that little sound again. It was even louder now.

Onyx noticed the fear in Amberly's eyes as she stared at the little satchel bag. "Oh, don't mind him. Buggles always does that."

"Buggles?" said Amberly.

"Yeah, Buggles is my little beetle bug."

Just then, a little purplish, black, shiny beetle popped his head out of Onyx's bag. He looked like one big, purple-black gem. Startled, Amberly jumped back. Safflower quickly darted behind Amberly's head and nuzzled into her hair. Then she managed the courage to peek over Amberly's shoulder and gaze at the little beetle curiously. She wasn't quite sure if it could be trusted since she had never seen a beetle quite like it before.

Onyx walked closer to Amberly and smiled. "So, what is that contraption behind your wing? Are those...twigs?" she said with a laugh. She tried to touch Amberly's wing brace, but Amberly quickly backed away.

Startled by Amberly's sudden move, Onyx flinched and gasped. "Sorry!" she said.

"It's ok," Amberly said reluctantly.

"Wait, is that a tiny wing in front of that contrap… I mean, wing-shaped twig? I've never seen anything like that before! Why is your little wing such an odd color?" Onyx said as she crinkled her nose. She wasn't aware how hurtful she was being despite her innocent curiosity.

"That's none of your business!" Amberly shouted forcefully and she began to walk away. She hadn't even a clue as to where she was going.

"Amberly, wait! I didn't mean to ask so many questions!" shouted Onyx as Amberly continued to walk away. "Stop! We must start our journey before it's too late!"

Amberly stopped in her tracks and turned on her heels to face Onyx. "Excuse me? What journey? I'm not going anywhere with you! This is the Dark Forest, isn't it?" Amberly stared at Onyx in confusion, somewhat irritated by Onyx's sudden forcefulness.

Onyx's saddened eyes looked as though they were about to tear up again. This little fairy had the most expressive face Amberly had ever seen. So much so that Amberly could almost feel exactly what Onyx was feeling.

"Some call our land the Dark Forest, but I just call it home," said Onyx.

Buggles belted out a high-pitched sort of a grunt and crawled back into Onyx's raven-feathered satchel. He was obviously bored with the conversation.

"My Uncle Orin warned me of this place," Amberly said nervously.

"Warned you? Warned you of the Dark Forest?" Onyx chuckled. "What could he have possibly warned you about in this boring place?"

Amberly's patience suddenly ran out and in a split second she leaned in toward Onyx's face. "I'm not here for small talk. I'm here to find my father, and I bet you know where he is!"

Onyx let out a loud gasp and stumbled backward a bit, all the while keeping her startled eye on Amberly. "I…I have no idea where your father is."

Amberly backed off a little. "I know you must have seen him. His wings are a blazing red and orange like the sun."

Onyx just shook her head nervously.

"I know he is here and I'm going to find him!" Amberly began to walk away from Onyx. Her determination was apparent.

Safflower kept a watchful eye on Onyx who was flying after them.

"Wait! Wait!" Onyx cried out. She was flying closely behind Amberly now but she couldn't seem to catch all the way up to her.

"Leave me alone!" shouted Amberly as she stopped and turned around to face Onyx again.

"But I can help you!" said Onyx.

Amberly stared at Onyx for a moment. Her patience had run dry so she looked Onyx right in the eye. "So, you do know where my father is!" I knew it!"

"Well, no. But, I know who can help."

Amberly continued to stare at Onyx, who had her full attention now.

"My Uncle Boggart can help. He is the greatest oracle of our land."

"Oracle?" Amberly asked curiously.

"Yes, a talented wizard. But, I really need your help with gathering a few ingredients my Uncle Boggart is going to need to create a special spell for me first."

Amberly looked at Onyx as if she'd lost her mind. "No way," she said and began to walk away again.

"Wait, Amberly! If you help me, I promise he will help you find your father!"

"How?" asked Amberly without even looking at Onyx, who continued flying behind her.

"He is a seer of all things," said Onyx.

Amberly stopped walking and turned around. She stared at Onyx intently. "I have an uncle who is a sorcerer, too. What exactly is this spell for?"

Onyx relaxed and let out a sigh of relief. She was finally getting through to Amberly. "It's for my grandfather. Something is terribly wrong with him. His legs have begun to fade away."

"Fade away?"

"Yes, his legs are vanishing. You can see right through them. It is the most peculiar sight to see. And his right arm is beginning to fade as well."

"Fade? But how?"

"We think it's some sort of a spell. But we have no idea why or how."

"And you're sure your Uncle Boggart can help your grandfather?"

Onyx's eyes lit up with a glimmer of hope. "Yes, but only if we bring him the ingredients that he needs to create the healing spell." She pulled out a dusty, tattered black notebook and opened it to the page with the healing spell ingredients written on it. "He needs sage, lava, and emeralds to be exact."

"So, you already know what you need. Why do you need my help?" Amberly asked.

"Well, to be honest, I'm too slow. And I'm a bit of a klutz. You seem like such an athletic fairy. You can swim, right?"

"Yes, I can swim. But, why do I need to know how to swim?"

"You'll find out soon enough."

"What?"

"Don't worry! If you help me, I'm sure my Uncle Boggart will help us find your father," said Onyx just as Amberly kicked a rock.

"And once we do this, your grandfather will be well?"

"Yes. It's his only hope."

"This Boggart…he will know where my father is?"

"Yes! I'm sure of it!" said Onyx.

Amberly pondered for a moment and stared at Onyx while Safflower flew all around them nervously. "Ok…I'll do it," she said.

Onyx clasped her hands together and let out a loud shriek. "Thank you! Thank you!" She was so overwhelmed with gratitude that she hugged Amberly tightly.

Amberly was startled by the sudden affection and just stood there stiffly while Onyx wrapped her in an embrace.

"So, where to now?" said Amberly.

"We must head south. First stop is the sage crops," said Onyx.

Amberly took a deep breath and sighed. Despite having had one sword fighting lesson with her Uncle Orin, and all the reading and studying about the Dark Forest she had accomplished, Amberly suddenly felt unprepared for this new adventure she was about to embark on.

Chapter Fourteen

Little Onyx flew as fast as she could in the direction of the sage crops while Amberly ran quickly behind her. Amberly's incredibly quick strides made it easy to keep up with Onyx, who was startled to see Amberly running quickly on the ground in front of her.

Onyx stopped abruptly and flew in one place for a moment. "What are you doing?"

"What's it look like I'm doing? I'm running."

"Running very fast I might add!" said Safflower as she sat on Amberly's shoulder.

Onyx stared at Amberly curiously while struggling to keep up with Amberly's quick stride. "But, you're a fairy…"

"Of course I'm a fairy."

"Then why aren't you flying? Does it have something to do with that contraption on your wing?"

"It's called a wing brace!" Amberly responded, and she started walking with quicker strides, causing Onyx to lag behind.

Suddenly, Amberly stopped in her tracks. Onyx stopped flying, landed right in front of Amberly, and stared at her intently.

"Fine," said Amberly. "If you must know, I was born with a paralyzed wing. I can't fly, and I lose my balance if I don't wear this *contraption* as you call it!"

Onyx blinked her eyes and took a step back. "I…I had no idea. I'm so sorry."

"It's called a wing brace. Safflower and I made it."

"You made it? That's amazing!"

"What's so amazing about it?" said Amberly. "Look, I don't want to talk. I just want to find my father."

Onyx was startled by Amberly's abrupt response but tried not to take offense. "Very well, then. I won't say a word. But it might be a good idea for us to be on friendly terms, since you have no idea where you're going in a land you've never been to before."

Safflower looked at Onyx curiously and then focused her attention on Amberly and said, "She does have a point, don't you think?"

Amberly shot an irritated glance at Safflower and continued to walk quickly. Safflower shrugged and began flying behind Onyx, who was utterly confused by Amberly's anger. Without saying a word, Onyx flew in front of Amberly while Safflower caught up and landed on Amberly's shoulder.

While Amberly followed Onyx, who was flying quickly in front of her in silence, her quick steps made it seem as though Amberly was gliding her feet effortlessly over the black soil and glittery silver rocks that glistened in the moonlight. There was something different about the moon in the Dark Forest. It seemed vividly brighter than Whimsical Land's moon and almost translucent. Amberly could see right through the moon that floated in the Dark Forest's sky. Onyx wasn't a very fast flyer, so Amberly had to force herself to slow down and let her lead the way since she had no idea where they were going.

Onyx looked back at Amberly every so often to make sure she was still there. Her big blue eyes were iridescent, and they seemed to sparkle in the moonlight when she turned her head just right.

"So, how far is this place we're going to?" Amberly asked.

"Uncle Boggart's castle is about ten fairy miles away. But first we have to stop at the sage crops," Onyx said. She stared back at Amberly while still flying forward.

Suddenly, out of nowhere, three blue trolls jumped from a black willow tree a few feet in front of Onyx. Before Amberly could warn her, Onyx bumped into one of the chubby trolls just after he had fallen from the tree. He landed on his back and poor Onyx fell right on top of the pudgy brute's stomach.

Amberly ran toward Onyx, who was trying to roll off the troll's stomach. It was no use. All Onyx could do was rock back and forth on the troll's chubby, blubbery, stomach with no success of escaping. Just as the troll was about to toss Onyx off his gut with his chubby hand, Amberly ran across his ugly chest. She picked Onyx up by the waist, tossed her into the air, and jumped off the troll's stomach. Onyx flew high above Amberly and the troll just in the nick of time as two more trolls fell from the tree and blocked Amberly's path.

Amberly froze while Onyx flew back down and landed on her feet next to Amberly and Safflower.

With their big red eyes and white, snaggly teeth that gleamed in the moonlight as they sported their evil smiles, the three ugly trolls stared intently at the fairies.

"What do you want?" Amberly screamed.

"Your sword, of course!" said the largest of the three trolls in a loud squeaky voice.

Amberly cringed at the unpleasant tone of this odd creature's voice and the troll laughed out loud, making her incredibly angry. "Come and get it, then!" she screamed as she threw her sword up in the air.

The three trolls ran toward Amberly, Onyx, and Safflower.

Onyx blurted out a spell as she held her hands out in front of her. "Make them see what cannot be, and summon flames that leap to make them flee! Make them hear what isn't there, their deepest worries come to bear!" she shouted.

A wall of flames rose up in front of the trolls, causing them to topple over each other. They all stumbled backward, away from the extreme heat emitting from the magnificent wall of fire. The flames grew so high that they looked as though they would surpass the treetops.

Amberly stood in awe of the large flames that Onyx had just

manifested. Safflower sat on Amberly's shoulder, with her tiny head nuzzling Amberly's neck.

"Onyx! Make it stop!" Amberly shouted as she shielded her eyes from the bright flames.

Onyx glanced at Amberly nervously and then focused her attention on the flames while raising both hands in the air slowly. Amberly watched Onyx closely and was amazed by the magic that Onyx had been able to conjure up.

"Wall of fire give up your power. Transform thyself to a tiny cower!" Onyx said sternly, causing the flames to shrink so low to the ground that they almost disappeared.

"Fire and flames, smolder no more, disappear into the dark night and leave nothing more!"

With that, the flames disappeared completely, leaving Amberly flabbergasted by what she had witnessed. She was so intrigued by what Onyx had just done that she almost forgot what they were doing there in the first place. Amberly suddenly snapped out of her daze, scooped Onyx up, hoisted her onto her back, and began to run as fast as she could. She jumped high above the trolls that were still rolling on the ground and coughing from the lingering smoke left by the giant wall of flames.

Chapter Fifteen

Amberly continued to run like a flash of lightning. She jumped in the air and glided a few feet, with Onyx still on her back holding on for dear life. Safflower was still nuzzled safely next to Amberly's neck, while Buggles was safely tucked away in Onyx's raven-feathered knapsack. Together, they sprinted and glided through the Dark Forest.

Still riding on Amberly's back, and pointing to the south, Onyx said, "This way to the sage crops!"

"Sage crops?" Amberly yelled out curiously.

"Yes, the first ingredient we must get for Grandfather's spell!"

Amberly sighed and dutifully ran in the direction that Onyx had pointed to. Soon they arrived at their first destination: the sage crops.

"We must grab a small bushel of sage and bring it to Uncle Boggart, but we have to be careful of the guards," said Onyx.

"The guards? What guards?" asked Amberly.

"The insect guards!"

"Insects?" Amberly said as she laughed at Onyx. "I think we can definitely outsmart a few insects!"

"But these insects are different, Amberly. They're smart and they're strong. We have to be careful not to wake them!"

"So, what are we waiting for?" Amberly started to walk quickly towards the crops.

"Wait!" Onyx said in a loud whisper, causing Amberly to stop in her tracks.

"What is it?" asked Amberly.

"We have to be very quiet. And, we need a plan."

"Ok. I'll cut the sage with my sword, and you catch the bundles as I cut."

"All right, On the count of three. One…two…three," whispered Onyx.

Amberly ran through the sage crop with sword in hand while Onyx flew a short distance behind her, desperately trying to keep up. Safflower held on tightly to Amberly's shoulder and kept on the lookout. Amberly cut the bundles of sage with her sword and tossed them behind her, and Onyx caught them.

An eerie, low fog hung over the sage crop, making it hard to see in the dim moonlight.

Safflower kept a close watch on the path ahead while she held on tightly to Amberly.

Looking ahead, she noticed a pair of green, glowing eyes hovering above the crops in the distance. Amberly and Onyx were moving so quickly that they didn't notice the stalking eyes until Safflower flew off Amberly's shoulder and yelled at the beetle guards to distract them.

"Hey! Over here! Bet you can't catch me!" Safflower shouted as she flew past the angry green eyes. Then, one by one, the strange-looking beetle guards began to chase Safflower.

"Amberly!" Onyx screamed. She pointed toward Safflower, who was flying away with the beetle guards trailing after her. Their tiny wings fluttered a mile a minute.

"Safflower! Come back! Come back!" Amberly screamed. She was terrified at the sight of the beetles catching up to Safflower.

Amberly ran so fast that she left Onyx behind. She could feel the muscles in her legs burn. She had never run so fast before in her whole, entire fairy life. And just as she caught up to Safflower, one of the beetles tugged Safflower's wing with its skinny little appendage and Safflower fell to the ground.

Amberly watched the scene in horror and screamed at the cruel beetle as she rushed to her little fairy butterfly's rescue. She scooped

Safflower up in her arms. "No!" Amberly cried as she hunkered down with Safflower beside a large stone. She cradled Safflower to her chest while waving her other hand above her head, desperately trying to shoo away the beetles that were now swarming above them.

Onyx flew as fast as her little wings could fly. Once she caught up to Amberly and Safflower, she pulled out a little bundle of sage from her satchel and recited another fire spell. "With this magic I now bestow, a flame to burn thee now, create the smoke to clear our path, and protect us from this evil wrath!" she shouted.

At that moment, the end of the sage bundle burst into a little flame. Onyx pursed her lips and blew out the flame, causing smoke to smolder where the flame had been. She quickly flew above Amberly and waved the bundle of sage in the air. The smoldering smoke enveloped the entire perimeter surrounding Amberly and Safflower.

One by one, the beetle bugs coughed and fell to the ground. Even though the angry insects were the sage-crop guardians, Onyx knew that the sage smoke would knock them for a loop. Beetles in the Dark Forest did not like smoke. Onyx knew this all too well because her own pet beetle had almost died after having been exposed to smoke from a fire that Onyx had magically created one day in her study room.

Buggles buried himself deep into Onyx's satchel and hid his face from remnants of smoke.

"Amberly! Run!" Onyx cried.

Amberly jumped up with Safflower in her arms and ran out of the sage crop. Onyx continued to wave her burning sage around, causing more beetle bugs to fall to the ground. Then she flew as fast as she could after Amberly. Once they finally found themselves far from the sage crop, Amberly spotted a cave and ran inside. Onyx flew into the cave right after her. She found Amberly sitting in the corner of the cave crying as she gently rubbed Safflower's tiny head.

"You're going to be ok, Saffy. I promise," Amberly said through the glittery, reddish-orange tears that fell like tiny drew droplets down her cheeks. The glow of her tears gave off a faint light that brightened the cave, which was only dimly lit by the moonlight. Safflower looked up at Amberly sadly but did not speak. Instead, she blinked slowly, her eyes still watering from feeling the intense pain from her torn wing.

Onyx walked slowly toward Amberly and Safflower and was deeply saddened at seeing poor Safflower hurt. "Amberly, how is she?"

Amberly shot a cold glance at Onyx. "How do you think she is? She's in pain!"

Onyx took another step forward cautiously. "I-I'm sorry."

"Don't be sorry. Do something!"

"But, I don't know what to do!"

Amberly stood up and leaned in close to Onyx's worried face. "You have to help her!" she shouted.

Onyx took a step back, startled by Amberly's intensely loud voice. "I…I don't know what I can do, Amberly!"

"What about a spell? Use one of your spells!"

Onyx knelt beside Safflower who slowly blinked her teary eyes. "I haven't been so lucky with using healing spells on Grandfather."

"If you can create a wall of fire, I'm sure you can heal a tiny butterfly wing!" said Amberly.

"I don't know…I…"

"Just try, Onyx! You just need to believe that you can, that's all! Don't be a coward!" shouted Amberly.

"I'm not a coward!" Onyx retorted angrily. She moved closer to Safflower and took a deep breath to calm her frazzled nerves.

Amberly stepped back to give Onyx some room and sat quietly with her legs crossed as she watched Safflower lying on the cave's dirt floor helplessly. Onyx closed her eyes and held her right palm over Safflower's head.

Suddenly, a blue light emanated from the palm of Onyx's hand. She placed her hand over Safflower's wing and chanted a healing spell. "By the full moon's light and helping hands, I spread good health throughout the lands. Send energies far and near to heal the wing of this fairy butterfly we hold dear!"

A blue light enveloped Safflower's entire body and much to Onyx's surprise, little Safflower began to flutter her wing! Suddenly, Safflower flew around the cave. She seemed to have more energy than before.

Amberly jumped to her feet, rushed over to Onyx, and threw her arms around her. She practically knocked her over. "You did it! Thank you! Thank you!" she shouted.

Onyx smiled and was completely shocked by Amberly's affection. "No biggy," she said. She winked at Safflower, who was flying in a circle above her head so fast that she looked like a sparkling, pinkish, purple ball of light flying quickly through the air.

"Woo hoo!" Safflower yelled as she laughed out loud. "I'm just as fast as you now, Amberly!"

Amberly smiled widely as she watched her little butterfly fly around the cave like a shooting star. "Amazing!" I don't know how to repay you!" she said to Onyx.

Onyx smiled bashfully as she pulled her mini-lantern from her knapsack and lit its wick with a magical snap of her fingers. She set the little lantern down, pulled out a few sticks from her never-ending knapsack full of surprises, and quickly arranged the sticks in a little pile. She held both hands palms down above the pile of sticks, and the sticks magically caught fire. There was finally a little warmth in the cave now.

"Nothing like a little campfire!" said Onyx with a grin.

"Campfire? I love campfires!" said Safflower as she flew above Amberly and finally landed on Amberly's shoulder with a thud. "Can we sing around the fire, Amberly? Can we? Can we?"

"Safflower? What's gotten into you?" You know I don't sing! Besides, we don't have time for that! Onyx, what's our next plan?" asked Amberly.

Onyx was startled by Amberly's demanding tone and flinched as she warmed her hands by the fire. She glanced over at Safflower, who looked very disappointed that Amberly was back to business already.

"Well, first, we must go to Emerald Falls at dawn," Onyx said as she pulled out a map that her grandfather had made for her from her knapsack.

Amberly moved closer to Onyx and sat next to her. She stared at the map intently while Onyx pointed to the little drawing of Emerald Falls on the map.

"Now, Emerald Falls is being guarded by the Emerald Fairy Guards."

"Fairies?" Amberly asked curiously with a glint of hope that other fairies would be easier to deal with than angry, violent, insects.

Onyx shook her head somberly.

"What is it?" Amberly asked curiously.

"These fairies are not like you and me."

"Why not?" asked Amberly.

Onyx just shuddered. "Well, they aren't the prettiest of beings. They're basically little vampires with wings!"

Safflower flinched in disgust. "Vampires?" she squealed.

"Yes..." Onyx moved closer to Amberly's shoulder and leaned in toward Safflower's tiny little face. "With fangs!" she said with a shriek in her voice.

It was so loud that Safflower fluttered her wings and flew up in the air in a hurry. She circled above Amberly and Onyx, who were laughing hysterically at her. Poor Safflower landed back on Amberly's shoulder and pouted. "Not funny."

"Aww...sorry Saffy."

"It's ok. At least I finally made you laugh," said Safflower.

"Hey! I always laugh!" said Amberly.

Safflower gave Onyx a look and shook her head from side to side.

"Anyway, don't listen to her," said Amberly. "Where do we find these vampire fairies with fangs and how do we get their emeralds?"

Onyx laid the map out over their laps. "First, we must get a very early start. As soon as the sun comes up."

"The sun actually comes up here in the Dark Forest?" asked Amberly.

"Well, somewhat. Anyway, we have to leave early."

"Where we going? Where we going?" Safflower shouted excitedly.

Amberly patted Safflower on the head to quiet her down while Onyx pointed to the area on the map that showed what looked like a beautiful sketch of a waterfall. Below the waterfall sketch was a drawing of shiny green emeralds piled at the bottom of the pond below the falls.

"Here it is. Emerald Falls. I've been there with my grandfather. We have to be quick once we get there."

"What do we do once we're there?" asked Amberly.

"We need four emeralds for the spell. You said you can swim, right?"

"Yes, of course."

"Perfect. I can't," Onyx replied. "I'm going to need you to dive to the bottom of the pond at the end of the falls and bring back four emeralds."

"The bottom of the pond?"

"No, Amberly! You can't!" said Safflower as she sat on Amberly's shoulder.

Amberly ignored Safflower. "I'll do it if you really think your uncle can help me find my father."

"But, that's dangerous, Amberly! You hardly ever swim!" Safflower protested.

Onyx looked at Amberly worriedly.

"I can do it," Amberly reassured her. "My legs and arms are strong. I'm a good swimmer!"

"Don't worry, the pond is not very deep," said Onyx. "And, I'm going to need your help too, Safflower."

Safflower looked at Onyx and Amberly nervously.

"No, we're not doing that again," said Amberly. "She's staying in your knapsack with Buggles."

Just then, Buggles popped his little head up and let out a happy squeal. Safflower flew over to Buggles and snuggled next to him inside the little knapsack.

"I'm good!" said Safflower.

Onyx sighed. "Ok, you and Buggles can help me make noise to distract the guards."

"How many of them?" asked Amberly.

"Three or four."

"But how are you supposed to distract all four vampire fairies without them seeing me?" asked Amberly.

Onyx quickly reached into her knapsack where Buggles and Safflower were snuggled in together. She pulled out a teensy, tiny burlap bag and opened it. "With cocoa beans!" she said as she poured a few beans out of the bag into Amberly's hand.

"Cocoa beans?"

"Yes, the skinny vampire fairy guards love cocoa beans. All you do is throw them and the ugly vampire fairy guards will fly right after them. That's what my grandfather used to do."

"Ok, if you say so," Amberly said reluctantly.

"Oh, and that's not all." Onyx said as she pulled out a tiny, corked glass bottle from her raven-feathered knapsack.

Amberly's eyes widened. "Really? How does all that stuff fit inside that little bag of yours?"

"Magic, of course!" Onyx said as she chuckled. "Anyway, once we get the emeralds, we must fly over to the Dark Forest's volcano and fill up this glass bottle with hot lava. Then that's it! We're done! No problem at all!"

"Wow. You make it sound so easy," said Amberly.

"Piece of cake! Now, get some rest. Your bed awaits you," said Onyx.

"What bed? You mean this cold cave floor?" said Amberly sarcastically.

"Not quite. Look behind you, Amberly."

Amberly turned around only to find a cozy little bed with two fluffy red pillows and a soft, rainbow-colored fleece blanket. "What?" she shouted with excitement. "How?" She ran and jumped right on top of the comfy little bed and removed her sword and wing brace with a smile. "Onyx! This is fairy awesome!"

Onyx laughed and then plopped herself down on the bed next to Amberly. Safflower and Buggles crawled out of Onyx's little knapsack, made their way between Amberly and Onyx, and snuggled together on the warm bed.

"Good night, Amberly," said Onyx with a yawn.

Amberly had already fallen asleep as soon as her head hit the pillow.

Onyx closed her eyes and all four were soon fast asleep, welcoming a much-needed rest before the challenging day ahead of them.

Chapter Sixteen

The Dark Forest's sunlight was brightest in the early morning hours. It definitely wasn't the same as the sunlight in Whimsical Land. The morning sun rays in this dark world were a kind of greyish, white color, and Amberly worried that she and Safflower stood out too much with their bright colors.

The foliage in this world was a somewhat murky, blackish-brown, and Amberly couldn't help but wonder what type of fruit the trees bore here. As she and Onyx walked through the dark vines and shrubs, her heart ached for Whimsical Land. She missed its warm sunlight and its colorful flowers and lush evergreen. She wondered if she would ever see her father, mother, and sister again.

Amberly continued to walk while Onyx and Safflower flew ahead of her. She usually liked to be the leader, but she was content at knowing Onyx knew the way to Emerald Falls.

With her sword, she cut a few black vines that had seemed to creep away from the trees and into their path. "How much farther is this place, anyway?"

"We're almost there."

"You promise?" said Safflower unconvinced.

"Promise," Onyx said as they continued to walk into the depths of the forest. Amberly thought about how much she missed the animals in Whimsical Land, especially the wolf pups. She noticed that the Dark Forest had none and she knew she could never live where there were no wolves. She even missed the chirping of Whimsical Land's birds. The Dark Forest was seemingly absent of birds and every other forest creature that existed back home.

A large green bug suddenly landed on Amberly's arm and startled her, causing her to flinch. Amberly swatted the bug off.

"Is that all you have in the Dark Forest? Bugs?"

Onyx laughed as Buggles let out a loud grunt as if to say he was offended by Amberly's rude inquiry. "Pretty much," she said. We do have some grasshoppers if you like those!"

"No thank you. I prefer butterflies and animals with fur," said Amberly.

"What animals have fur?"

"Wolves, squirrels, deer, bears, and rabbits of course."

"I would love to see those one day," said Onyx. "What is fur, anyway?"

"It's kind of like short, fuzzy, thick hair that covers the animal's body," said Amberly.

Just then, Onyx abruptly stopped flying. "Shhh!" she said as she motioned for Amberly and Safflower to hide behind the lush, brownish-green shrubbery. As they peeked through the shrubs, they could see a huge waterfall in the valley below them. Amberly stared at the waterfall. It was incredibly beautiful. The pond below it was riddled with emeralds and glittery grey rocks that glistened in the pale sunlight beneath the grey sky. The waterfall shimmered and sparkled as it poured into the glittery pond.

"Emerald cove?" asked Amberly.

"How'd you guess?" Onyx said with a grin.

"Where are the guards? I don't see anyone. Now's our chance!" Amberly said as she began to move forward through the shrubs.

"Look!" said Onyx as she pointed to the vampire fairy guard that had just emerged from behind a boulder at the edge of the pond. Amberly shuddered at the sight of him and gasped. She had never seen such an ugly fairy before. Safflower popped her head out of

Onyx's raven feathered knapsack and let out a tiny scream when she saw the vampire fairy down below next to the pond. She couldn't bear to look at the male fairy's fangs, grey skin, and green scraggly hair. His scrawny wings were a moldy green and his skin was covered with little green bumps and lumps all over it. His white fangs stood out as they protruded from his red lips while his piercing red eyes looked up toward the small hill where Onyx and Amberly stood.

"That is the most God-awful fairy I have ever seen in my life!" said Amberly.

"Tell me about it," said Onyx. "Are you ready to run?"

Amberly nodded while Safflower and Buggles tucked themselves back inside Onyx's knapsack and let out two little gasps. "Let's get this over with," she said.

Onyx nodded her head and flew down toward the pond. Amberly did her usual routine, switching back and forth between running and gliding in the air a few seconds at a time. She desperately wanted to pass Onyx by but refrained from moving ahead of her since she was in a foreign land and didn't want to interfere with Onyx's plan, whatever that was. All she knew was that she was going to have to dive into the pond and grab four emeralds. Amberly slowed down as Onyx motioned for her to hide behind a large weeping willow tree at the edge of the pond. She noticed the vampire fairy was walking along the edge of the pond with his back turned to them.

Amberly watched the vampire fairy as he stood on the side of the pond, staring off to the east. She was curious to know what the strange fairy was staring at. Then she saw it. It was a huge volcano off in the distance behind the waterfall. Amberly was mesmerized by what she was witnessing. She had never seen a volcano before. She had heard that they existed in faraway lands but she'd never thought she would see one in her lifetime. She was entranced by the slow trickle of the lava that flowed down the volcano's side and into a deep pit below.

Onyx waived at Amberly and let out a soft whisper. "Amberly…"

Amberly snapped out of her entrancement with the volcano and paid attention to Onyx, who motioned for Amberly to stay where she was. Then, Onyx flew quickly toward the side of the pond where the vampire fairy stood and whistled loudly. The ugly little vampire fairy turned his head with a jerk and caught sight of Onyx hovering over the side of the pond.

"Hey you! Mr. Red Eyes!" You want some?" Onyx yelled as she pulled the cocoa beans from her raven-feathered knapsack. Vampire fairies loved the taste of cocoa beans. They considered them a delicacy, and it was rare that vampire fairies would ever get to sink their teeth into fresh cocoa beans.

The ugly vampire fairy's eyes widened, and he let out an angry snarl.

"Come on! Come and get it!" shouted Onyx.

The angry vampire fairy suddenly flew toward Onyx. Amberly gasped. Just as the vampire fairy flew closer to Onyx, Onyx threw the handful of cocoa beans far into the forest and the vampire fairy flew after them, disappearing into the woods.

Amberly ran toward the pond and dove into the glittery, chilly green waters. She swam toward the bottom of the pond and found piles and piles of sparkling green emeralds covering the glittery pond's floor. She quickly grabbed two emeralds with each hand and held them tightly in her fists as she swam.

The pond was still and calm until Amberly suddenly felt a strong current behind her. As she swiftly turned herself around under water, she was startled by a school of strange fish. As they swam closer, Amberly could see their gnashing teeth and angry, yellow eyes. They were piranha fish and they were headed straight for her!

Amberly kicked her legs and swam as fast as she could through the green waters with the school of fish at her heels. Although she could glide through the waters with the speed of an arrow, one of the fish caught up to her and snapped at her feet. Amberly swam even faster.

Onyx watched in terror. She saw the piranha fish gaining speed just as Amberly made it to the water's edge. "Amberly! Are you ok?"

she shouted as Amberly quickly jumped out of the pond and sat at the water's edge to catch her breath.

Amberly anxiously touched her wing brace, but to her pleasant surprise, it was still intact. "Really? You didn't think to warn me about the killer fish?' she shouted.

Onyx shook her head no. "I'm so sorry! I had no idea! That never happened when grandfather dove into that pond a few years ago!"

Onyx looked up and then shouted, "Amberly, get up! Hurry! We have to go!" She pointed at the angry vampire fairy flying toward them.

Amberly jumped to her feet and ran after Onyx, who flew as fast as she could toward the direction of the volcano. The two glanced back at the angry vampire fairy running after them. He was belting out throaty, frog-like sounds.

Amberly continued to run behind Onyx until the vampire fairy finally stopped running and shook his fists in the air. He was utterly defeated as he watched Amberly and Onyx disappear into the Dark Forest.

Chapter Seventeen

Amberly and Onyx made it safely to the Dark Forest's volcano, where they stopped next to what looked like a big pile of volcanic rocks. As Amberly looked closer, she noticed that the rocks were piled high and took on the shape of a little hut. There was a small opening at the base of the rocks where Onyx slipped inside. Amberly followed right behind her. She was a bit nervous because the rock hut looked as if someone or something lived in there, however, at least for that moment, Onyx and Amberly could rest their tired wings and legs.

Even so, Amberly still wanted to check the place out. She wasn't sure it was safe—she really wasn't sure about anything anymore. "What is this place? How do you know we're the only ones in here?"

"I don't," said Onyx.

Amberly pulled out her sword and crept around, looking behind every random rock and stone within the hut.

"Relax, Amberly," Onyx said, and she laughed. "The last time, when Grandfather and I were here, this hut was abandoned." She sat down on what looked like a chair made of stones and leaned her head back on the rocky wall. "Looks like everything is still the same as before. Nothing's moved, so I think we're safe."

Amberly lowered her sword and placed it back in its scabbard. She walked toward Onyx and sat down in another little stone chair next to her. Safflower and Buggles popped their heads out of Onyx's knapsack, which was sitting on the ground at Onyx's feet.

Amberly noticed that there was a huge stone in front of what looked somewhat like a fireplace. She didn't want to get her hopes up. All she knew at that point was that she was freezing and a fireplace would be heaven. "What is that?" she asked.

"What is what?" Onyx asked curiously.

"That! Behind that stone!"

"I…I'm not sure. I've never been able to move that huge rock out of the way," said Onyx.

Amberly jumped up out of her stone chair and rushed over to the huge rock. With both hands she pushed the large stone and rolled it over a few feet.

"Amberly, look! A fireplace!" shouted Onyx.

Amberly's eyes widened and she smiled for the first time since arriving at the dark forest.

"How did you do it? That rock was impossible to move!" Onyx said.

Amberly shrugged. "It's no big deal."

"No big deal? Why didn't you tell me you had a magical gift, Amberly?"

Amberly shot an irritated glance at Onyx. "I don't have a magical gift!"

Onyx flinched and backed away from Amberly. "Oh. I'm sorry. I…I've just never seen a fairy as strong as you before."

"Well, now you have. I know it's weird, so don't look at me that way."

"I don't think it's weird. I think it is amazing! An especially useful gift, actually!"

"I don't want to talk about it anymore!" Amberly protested.

"Ok, fine." Onyx desperately tried not to say another word, but she just couldn't help herself. "I mean, I don't understand why you're so angry. I wish I were as strong as you."

"No, you don't. Trust me. You are better off being able to fly."

"Yeah, but…"

"But nothing!" said Amberly, irritated. "I'm cold. Will you build a fire, please?"

"Sure," said Onyx. She reached inside her little knapsack, which had Safflower and Buggles still in it, and she pulled out ten dry twigs and placed them in the dusty fireplace. She shuffled through her bag again, pulled out Buggles, and sat him down next to Amberly. Safflower flew out of the knapsack and sat on Amberly's shoulder.

"Sorry little ones. I need my pebbles." Onyx searched through her knapsack once more. "Ahh! Here they are!" she said as she pulled out a few pebbles from the knapsack and arranged them in a circle around the twigs. Amberly watched Onyx curiously while the little purple-haired fairy closed her blue eyes and chanted a fire spell while holding her left hand above the twigs.

"May the twigs beneath my hand smolder into burning flames. So be it. So it is!" Onyx chanted. Suddenly, a flicker of a flame appeared on top of one of the twigs. In an instant, the whole bundle of twigs caught on fire, which made Amberly smile again.

"How do you do that?" she asked.

Onyx blushed and patted Buggles on the head after he crawled up her leg and rested in her lap. She took out the map again from her knapsack and unfolded it. Amberly looked out of the little hut's door and saw the Dark Forest's volcano in the distance.

"Next stop on our list," said Onyx as she pointed to the volcano on the map.

"Oh, great. Now what do I have to do?" asked Amberly.

"Not much. Just need you to fill these two little glass bottles with hot lava, remember?" Onyx said as she pulled out the tiny bottles from her knapsack. "No big deal, really."

"No big deal? This actually sounds worse than that piranha pond!" said Amberly with concern.

"But, don't you want to find your father?"

"Of course I do! I just don't know why I have to do all these dangerous stunts for you."

Onyx let out a loud sigh and lowered her head. "Because, I'm…"

Amberly interrupted impatiently. "You're what?"

"I'm too slow. And I'm not strong! You are though! You've definitely proven that! Besides, my grandfather said someone who could do anything was going to be sent to help me and here you are! Look, all you have to do is collect the lava without the lava queen seeing you."

Amberly shook her head with concern. "How am I supposed to fill those tiny bottles up with hot lava without burning my hands?"

"With these!" Onyx said as she pulled out two gloves from her knapsack and handed them to Amberly.

"What am I supposed to do with these? Hot lava will burn right through these gloves!" said Amberly disappointedly.

Onyx shook her head. "No! You really think I would give you just any old gloves? These are my grandfather's gloves!" said Onyx excitedly.

Amberly leaned back and sighed. "Let me guess. These are magic gloves, right?"

"Of course they are! All you need to do is put these on, dunk the two glass bottles in the lava to fill them up, and you won't feel a thing. No heat whatsoever!"

Amberly just stared at Onyx. She was still a little unconvinced, but what other choice did she have other than to believe what Onyx was telling her. Besides, she had made up her mind that she would do anything if it meant there was a chance of her finding her father. "Well, if you say so," she said.

Onyx looked at Amberly sympathetically. "You know, you really do need to start trusting me." She chuckled. You're wearing me out!"

Amberly let out a big sigh just as Onyx held out her right hand, palm face-up and snapped her fingers with her left hand. Amberly flinched and let out a gasp when she noticed berries and nuts had just appeared in Onyx's hand right before her eyes.

"Berry?" said Onyx as she held her handful of berries and nuts in front of Amberly's nose.

Thank you! I'm starving. How did you...? Oh, never mind," said the awed Amberly as she scooped a few berries from Onyx's hand.

"Ok, fine. I trust you, but how am I supposed to fill these glass bottles without the lava queen seeing me?"

"You just have to be incredibly quiet. The lava queen is known to sleep a lot. Don't worry. You'll be fine."

"Oh, ok. Actually, I'm a little tired myself. I'd like to go to sleep now," said Amberly somberly as Onyx stared at her blankly.

"Well…aren't you going to magically make us a place to sleep or something?" Amberly asked with a grin.

"Oh! Yes, of course!" With that, Onyx swirled her hand in a circular motion and a soft bed of feathers and wool appeared on the little lava rock hut's floor. A beautiful, knitted turquoise blanket lay on top of it. Amberly jumped into the little bed and slid under the blanket, letting her body melt into a relaxing state as she fell fast asleep. Safflower flew down beside her, smiled at Amberly, and then watched Onyx, who was still studying the map by the fire.

Tomorrow was going to be a big day. The lava was the last element they needed for the spell to heal her grandfather, and with Boggart's help, Amberly was going to find her father. Onyx was sure of it.

Chapter Eighteen

The night flew by and the Dark Forest's sunrays made their way through the grey morning sky and lit up the little volcanic rock hut with a dim light. Amberly rolled over in the soft feather bed and awoke to Onyx standing over her, wide eyed and chipper.

"Good morning sleepyhead!" said Onyx. "You ready to meet the lava queen? I mean, well, hopefully you don't meet her. That was a joke. Sorry. Bad joke."

Amberly opened her eyes and then quickly closed them again. She covered her head with her hands.

"We have to go before the lava queen awakes," said Onyx.

Amberly opened her eyes and sat up. "Show me the way."

The morning air was chilly and the sky was still cloudy and grey as Amberly walked quickly behind Onyx, who was flying a few feet in front of her. They were headed for the volcano, which was now just a half a mile away. Safflower fluttered her wings and flew off Amberly's shoulder when she spotted a patch of dark-purple, orchid-like flowers glistening with morning dew. It was the first sighting of any colorful flowers that she and Amberly had seen since their traumatic arrival in the Dark Forest. Safflower landed on one of the flowers and sipped its nectar. She noticed that this flower's nectar tasted different than any of the flowers she had tasted in Whimsical Land.

"Hmmm. Not bad. But I've had better," Safflower said as she flew back to Amberly's shoulder and sat.

"You know what I miss the most?" asked Amberly.

"What?" Onyx asked.

"The butterwort?" said Safflower.

"Uh huh. They are Whimsical Land's most beautiful lilac and white flower."

"Ahh yes. How could I forget! They are delicious, too," said Safflower sadly.

"We will be home soon, Safflower, I promise you," Amberly comforted her.

At that moment, Onyx flew quickly behind a large, grey, stone pile and called out to Amberly. "Over here! Hurry!"

With Safflower on her shoulder, Amberly ran toward Onyx and ducked behind the pile of stones with her.

"Look!" Onyx said as she pointed toward the volcano. They were very close to the magnificent sight, yet a little frightened at the same time. They watched the bright-red, molten lava slowly creeping and oozing down the side of the volcano. At the very top of the volcano's peak was the lava queen's castle, which was made of lava stone.

"What if she sees me?" asked Amberly.

"She won't. She usually sleeps all day and stays awake all night. Her guards, well, that's a different story."

"Guards? You didn't mention anything about her having any guards."

"Well, of course she does. All queens have guards, Amberly," said Onyx.

Amberly sighed and shook her head. "Ok, never mind. Just tell me when to go. I want to get this over with!"

Onyx quickly pulled out the two little glass bottles from her knapsack and handed them to Amberly as Safflower looked on curiously. "Fill these up with as much lava as you can."

Amberly nodded in agreement as she listened intently to Onyx.

"Oh! Don't forget these! Here, put them on." Onyx handed Amberly the magic gloves. "Don't worry. I'll watch for the guards.

Go now, Amberly. Run! Don't look back!" she said in a hushed voice as she opened her knapsack and motioned for Safflower to hop inside.

"Ok, see you soon!" Amberly whispered back.

With a start, Amberly ran toward the row of lava rocks that led to the pool of smoldering lava. She quickly hopped across each rock and kept her balance every time she landed. She was so agile and strong. With the help of her wing brace she balanced herself with ease. Yet, at the same time she desperately tried to calm her nerves since she was aware of the hot lava rumbling in front of her once she made it to the large lava pool that bubbled and fizzed in front of the volcano.

Amberly looked up at the lava queen's castle and all was quiet. She carefully crouched down to reach the lava percolating at the base of the volcano, hoping she would never catch sight of the evil fairy queen who lived there.

She reached for the tiny glass bottles tucked away in her satchel and then dunked them into the lava. Just as Onyx had promised, Amberly's hands did not burn. She was amazed that she felt no heat whatsoever on her hands. Once the little glass bottles were filled with lava, she placed their tiny cork caps back on them and then safely secured them inside her satchel bag.

Onyx looked on nervously as she kept a close eye on Amberly's surroundings. Suddenly, a group of arrows darted right above Onyx, headed straight for Amberly. It was the lava queen's guards! In a flash, Onyx outstretched her hand and with her magic created fiery arrows that shot out from the palm of her hand and incinerated the wooden arrows headed for Amberly.

"Amberly! Run!" Onyx screamed as she fought off more arrows with her magic fire spell.

Amberly hastily looked up above. The sky was riddled with flaming arrows colliding with the wooden arrows, which exploded instantaneously and disintegrated into the air one by one.

Amberly quickly ran back across the rocks and joined Onyx, who was waiting for her on the other side of the volcano behind a boulder.

"Hurry!" Onyx shouted as she flew in the opposite direction of the volcano.

Amberly ran after her, catapulted herself into the air, grabbed Onyx's hand, and then motioned for Onyx to jump on to her back. "Which way?" she shouted.

Onyx pointed to a group of large oak trees with black branches and thick, black and grey leaves. "Head for the trees!"

With Onyx on her back, Amberly ran through to the other side of the Dark Forest, which seemed a bit darker than the rest of the forest. The foliage in this area looked like thick, black, rope-like, curly vines, which cascaded down from the tall, thick trees' branches all the way down to the ground.

As Amberly slowed down and let Onyx jump off her back, she noticed mushrooms scattered all around the trunks of every tree. There was something about these mushrooms that caught Amberly's eye. They were not like the mushrooms in Whimsical Land—these mushrooms were extremely glossy. With their shiny red caps covered with tiny white dots and shiny white stems, the mushrooms shimmered and sparkled like little pieces of stained glass. Amberly was completely drawn to them. Their brightness was beautiful and she was pleasantly surprised to find more color in the Dark Forest.

She walked toward one of the mushrooms resting near the tree trunk closest to her. As she moved in closer and reached down to touch it, Onyx turned around and let out a loud gasp.

"Amberly! No! Those mushrooms are poisonous!"

Amberly stopped herself from reaching for the glassy red and white spotted mushroom and walked over to Onyx. "But they're so beautiful."

"Please tell me you didn't touch it!"

"Relax. I didn't."

"Thank the heavens!" said Onyx with a sigh of relief. "Hurry, we must make it to Uncle Boggart's soon. He hates when visitors interrupt his dinner. But, if we make it there before dinner time, he will gladly share his meal with us."

"How do you know he'll share his dinner? He doesn't even know me," Amberly asked.

"He always shares whatever he's eating. My uncle loves to cook. He'll have plenty."

Onyx flew ahead of Amberly and they passed another area of the Dark Forest that seemed to have more of a greyish tinge to the foliage and trees. The leaves on the trees in this area were lined with fuzzy black edges. Amberly was in awe. She most definitely had never seen anything like this place before.

Chapter Nineteen

Off in the distance there stood a dark-purple castle. Amberly stopped for a moment and stared at the magnificent castle glistening in the soft grey sunset.

Onyx froze in mid-flight and looked back at Amberly, who was standing still and obviously mesmerized by the castle in front of them. "Come on Amberly! Hurry up! We're almost there!"

Amberly leapt into the air, somersaulted, and caught up to Onyx in a flash. "Is that your Uncle Boggart's castle?"

Onyx chuckled gleefully. "Of course! Now, hurry up."

As Onyx began to fly straight toward the castle once again, Safflower and Buggles peeked out of the little knapsack hanging snugly over her shoulder.

Amberly ran closely behind them with a hint of excitement in her heart. "I'm really not very hungry," she said.

Onyx stopped in mid-flight once again. As she paused in place, Amberly leapt into the air and her head accidently bumped Onyx's feet.

"Ouch!" Amberly said when she fell to the ground and landed on her backside. "What'd you stop for?"

"Amberly, listen to me, if my uncle offers you something to eat, be polite and eat it, ok?"

"Why?"

"Ok, there's something I have to tell you," said Onyx.

Amberly crossed her arms and stared at Onyx suspiciously. "I knew there was a catch! What is it?"

Onyx slowly floated down next to Amberly and sighed. "There's no catch. You just need to know that my uncle is not always the nicest fairy in the world. He's started fights with my grandfather over the years and I haven't always liked him because of this. I put up with him when I have to."

Amberly pulled her sword out of her scabbard and cut one of the black, curly, spiral vines off the tree that they were standing next to. "Great. I hope we don't have to stay long." She raised her voice. "And if he isn't very kind, what makes you think he will want to help me find my father?"

Onyx began to fly in the air again. "He will be nice to you. He just says mean things to my grandfather sometimes. I hate it. I think he's just jealous of my grandfather. Brotherly rivalry, I guess. He will help us, though. I promise. He's more interested in stranger fairies than his own family," she said with an irritated tone.

"So, if he is mean to his family, why will he concoct a spell for your grandfather, the brother that he fights with?"

"Because, even though he can be cruel to his own brother, he hates to see him sick or physically hurt."

Amberly shook her head and shrugged disappointedly. "Wow, he has issues."

"Just eat whatever he offers you. He will be insulted if you don't try his cooking, and if he's insulted then we won't get what we need from him. But, don't worry, he will help you."

Extremely irritated now, Amberly stood still and nodded. "Ok, ok...Let's just get there already."

"All right, hurry up then!" Onyx said, and she began to fly toward the castle with Amberly following closely behind her.

Amberly had no idea what to expect as they walked up to the castle door. Onyx knocked on the wooden door loudly with her fist as Safflower flew out of Onyx's raven-feathered knapsack and landed on Amberly's shoulder.

"Remember what I said, Amberly. Just accept his food even if you're not hungry, got it?" said Onyx.

"I know! I know!" Amberly snapped.

Onyx sighed and tapped her foot impatiently. She shouted, "Where is that uncle of mine?" as she lifted the handle on the black, iron, dragon-faced doorknocker that hung on the castle's purple door. Onyx slammed the knocker up and down on the door while Amberly covered her ears.

"Uncle Boggart!" Onyx screamed at the top of her lungs. She had begun to knock once again when the door finally opened. It was Boggart.

Amberly gasped. She was startled by the old male fairy that stood before them. He wasn't what she had expected. Boggart was much shorter than any of the male fairies in Whimsical Land. He was only as tall as Onyx, who was significantly shorter than Amberly. His hair was black and grey, his complexion was as pale as Onyx's, and his thick wings were a deep, dark, purple with black, silky spots scattered all over them. He wore a tattered, black, purple, and silver paisley-designed shirt, black pants, and a crown made of black feathers embedded with purple-amethyst gemstones.

"Onyx! What a wonderful surprise! Come in! Come in!" said Boggart. He gasped when he saw Amberly and he shielded his eyes from her bright-red hair and reddish-orange wing when she followed Onyx into the castle's foyer.

"Uncle Boggart, this is my friend, Amberly."

"How do you do?" said Amberly as she shook Boggart's hand.

"What a beautiful creature you are!" said Boggart. "Oh, dear… What happened to your wing?"

Embarrassed by Boggart's question, Amberly pulled her hand from his grip and her cheeks flushed red as she looked down at the floor.

"She was born that way, Uncle," said Onyx curtly.

"Oh, you poor thing. Does it hurt?" Boggart said as he reached out his hand to touch Amberly's paralyzed wing. Amberly quickly moved behind Onyx to assure she was out of Boggart's reach.

"Amberly's wing is paralyzed. It doesn't matter, though, because she is stronger than any of us," said Onyx.

"Really?" said Boggart.

Amberly shook her head no. She desperately wanted Onyx to change the subject. "I'm not that strong," she said under her breath.

"Amberly isn't from around here, Uncle Boggart." said Onyx.

"Clearly she is not. Are you a…a Whimsical?" asked Boggart with a grin.

Amberly nodded her head, yes, and Boggart stared at her in awe. Amberly shot a glance at Onyx, silently begging her to make Boggart stop staring.

"But, how did you end up here?" he asked curiously.

Amberly just shrugged and didn't say a word. It was as if Boggart's attention on her paralyzed wing had shut her down completely. The shame she felt because of her paralyzed wing was debilitating and she was at a loss for words.

The three were still standing in the foyer while Boggart shut the castle door and stared at Amberly in shock.

"Uncle Boggart, I…I'm here to request a spell for grandfather, and…" Onyx babbled on so fast that Boggart blinked his eyes quickly and stepped back.

"Whoa! Whoa! Slow down there. That's my niece for you," Boggart said as he nudged Amberly's side, causing her to back away, irritated. "Please, come join me in the dining room. You're just in time for dinner. I have plenty of food."

Onyx smiled at her uncle. "Of course, Uncle. We would love something to eat. We're famished. Aren't we, Amberly?" She looked at Amberly and gave her a hard nudge on the arm.

"Oh, uh, yes, famished," Amberly said as she cleared her throat.

Boggart's eyes brightened. "Perfect! Follow me!" he said as he walked ahead of Onyx and Amberly.

Onyx followed behind her uncle and smiled back at Amberly. The two were trying desperately not to laugh as they walked through the large castle's hallway. Boggart seemed harmless enough, Amberly thought to herself.

The three made their way to the dining room table where Boggart politely pulled a chair away from the long table. He motioned for Amberly to have a seat. Safflower suddenly flew out of Onyx's knapsack and sat on Amberly's shoulder while Buggles stayed behind and continued to hide in Onyx's knapsack.

"Thank you," Amberly said.

"Thanks, Uncle Boggart!" said Onyx.

"My pleasure, dear ones." said Boggart. "What a beautiful butterfly you have there!"

"Thank you. This is Safflower," said Amberly.

"Nice to meet you, Safflower," Boggart said with a smile.

Safflower smiled sweetly without saying a word.

Amberly looked around the grand feast that was before them and the large, extravagant dining room. The room was ten times larger than the little fairy cottage she'd grown up in, but oh, how she missed her little cottage right now. She thought about her mother and Calista and how they must be worried sick about her. She felt guilty even eating, because she knew her mother would not be eating her own dinner. Her mother never ate when she was upset.

Amberly brought her attention back to the present moment and admired Boggart's large, black, potbelly stove and the myriad of little copper pots and pans that hung on the walls in such a way that they looked like one giant art piece. She watched Boggart flutter back and forth from the kitchen's stone counter, which was covered with several plates and beautifully prepared soufflés and soups. He fluttered back and forth from the kitchen to the dining room table and placed the little bowls of soups, soufflés and sweet, colorful cakes in front of Amberly and Onyx.

"Blueberry flambé?" Boggart said as he held an iron pan.

"Yes, please. I love blueberries," said Amberly sadly.

"Thank you, Uncle Boggart. This looks delicious," said Onyx while Boggart placed flower-blossom soup and honey cakes on the table.

"Anyone care for lavender tea?"

"Umm…" Amberly said hesitantly.

Seeing Amberly's reluctance, Onyx kicked Amberly under the table.

"Ouch!" Amberly said under her breath and quickly got the hint. "Sure. Love some."

Amberly disliked the taste of lavender and she remembered her mother trying to get her to drink lavender tea when she was just a whimsy.

"*It's good for you, Amberly!*" her mother would say. But no matter how much her mother tried, Amberly would not drink it for the life of her. Now she took a sip of Boggart's tea and tried not to grimace. "Thank you," she said somewhat convincingly.

Boggart sat down and set his napkin in his lap. "So, my little niece, what brings you here, today?"

Onyx wiped her mouth with her little napkin. "Well, like I said, it's grandfather."

"Oh dear. What has that brother of mine done now?"

"Nothing. He's done nothing. He's been hexed with a terrible spell of some sort."

"A spell?"

"Yes, his legs have disappeared! And now his right arm is disappearing as well!"

"Disappearing? My poor brother!"

"We brought you a few gifts. Grandfather knows it's always been difficult for you to get your spell ingredients because of all the fairy guards guarding the elements, so, we brought you sage, emeralds, and lava."

Boggart's eyes widened with excitement. "My dear niece, you are one of a kind! A true gem! Of course I'll concoct a spell for my poor brother." He lifted his tiny porcelain teapot and poured some lavender tea into Onyx's mug. Amberly watched him curiously.

Boggart eyed her back. "And you, Miss Amberly?"

"Yes?" Amberly said as she continued to chew a bite full of berries.

"I'm sensing that there's something that has brought you here as well," said Boggart.

Before Amberly could respond, Onyx quickly butted in. "Amberly is looking for her father!"

"Your father?" Boggart asked curiously

"Yes," Amberly said sadly. "He's been missing since I was two." With a tinge of anger in her voice she added, "And I know who's captured him."

"I'm not following," said Boggart.

Onyx quickly jumped in. "Someone or something kidnapped her father and Amberly says it's one of the Dark Forest's fairies that took him!"

Amberly nodded her head. "Yes, I know it was one of the dark fairies. My Uncle Orin calls them the Band of Nyxies."

Boggart stared at Amberly for a moment and then suddenly let out a boisterous laugh.

"What's so funny?" shouted Amberly.

Boggart laughed even harder now.

"Uncle Boggart! This is no laughing matter!" Onyx yelled.

"The Band of Nyxies?" Boggart said as he tried to tone down his laughter. "Why, there's no such thing as the Band of Nyxies!"

Amberly slammed both her fists on the table. "There is so!" she yelled.

"Hogwash! The old fables about the Band of Nyxies are just legends. Bedtime stories, to say the least. They just don't exist, Amberly. I'm sorry," said Boggart.

Amberly stared at Boggart. Tears began to well up in her eyes. "No...but, that doesn't make any sense," she said softly.

Boggart cleared his throat, took a sip of his lavender tea, and then slowly set his tiny porcelain teacup down onto its saucer. "I'm very sorry for your loss," he said sincerely and looked away sadly.

"No!" Amberly screamed at the top of her lungs as she quickly stood up.

Onyx jumped at the sound of Amberly's fists hitting the wooden tabletop.

Boggart desperately tried to catch the honey cakes that had been piled on a silver plate and were now airborne from the force of Amberly's strong blow. He caught three of them but missed what seemed like a half a dozen, which landed haphazardly on the tabletop. "What in heaven's name?" he cried.

Onyx touched Amberly's arm, which was still trembling with anger as she stared at Boggart in shock.

"How dare you? The band of Nyxies does exist! And you're going to help me find them!" shouted Amberly.

Boggart blinked his eyes and suddenly let out another boisterous laugh. "Help you? How can I help you find something that is nowhere to be found except in that crazy imagination of yours!"

Amberly looked at Onyx with tears in her eyes, silently begging Onyx to do something...anything.

"Uncle Boggart, surely you could try to help us. Don't you think there might be a slight chance you could be wrong? I mean, maybe Amberly's Uncle Orin is right!" said Onyx.

"Nonsense. Come now, both of you. Finish your dinners so that we can start making that spell of yours, Onyx."

Amberly just stood there feeling defeated while hot, salty tears rolled down her cheeks. Safflower felt so bad for her. She moved closer to Amberly's face and fluttered her tiny wing against Amberly's cheek, wiping away her tears.

"Thanks for nothing," Amberly said to Onyx, and then she started to walk away from the table.

Onyx flew over to Amberly and grabbed her arm. "Wait! Where are you going?"

"To find my father!" Amberly pulled her arm from Onyx's grip and started to run out of the dining room with Safflower holding onto her shoulder as tightly as she could.

Onyx quickly flew after her. "Amberly!" she said as she caught up to Amberly and grabbed onto her arm again.

"Let go of me!" Amberly shouted.

"Wait! Don't go! I'll just need to make this spell for Grandfather, and then I'll go with you!"

"Don't bother. I…I can't even trust you anymore!" With that, Amberly continued to run out of the large dining room.

"Amberly, wait!" shouted Onyx as she flew toward Amberly.

"Don't follow me, Onyx! I never want to see you again!"

Onyx stopped in midair and floated back down to the floor. She was shocked by Amberly's harsh words. Glittery purple tears sparkled as they rolled down her cheeks and she glared at her uncle who just sat there, sipping on his tea.

"We have to stop her, Uncle Boggart! She needs our help!"

Boggart calmly took a bite of a honey cake then motioned for Onyx to sit back down. "She won't get very far. Don't worry."

Onyx stared angrily at her uncle and shouted, "What are you talking about? We need to help her!"

"Trust me, dear one. She can't go far, it's not possible." Boggart smiled and gave Onyx a wink.

"Uncle Boggart? What have you done?"

"Nothing but a little magic, I suppose."

Chapter Twenty

Amberly ran through the castle's corridors and headed for the front entrance door. She pulled on the castle door's handle, but to her utter surprise, it wouldn't budge. Again, she tried to pull the door open, but still, no luck.

Fluttering above Amberly's head, Safflower looked on nervously. "You can do it, Amberly!"

"Come on, open up!" Amberly shouted angrily as she continued to try to turn the stubborn knob on the door. "Your magic is no match for me, Boggart!" Using all the strength she had, she placed her left foot on the castle's stone wall beside the door to steady herself and pulled the door's handle with every ounce of strength she had left in her tiny fairy body. But, it was no use, the door would not open.

Amberly realized that Boggart's magic really *was* a match for her strength and that thought was too much for her to bear. Feeling defeated, she slowly let herself fall to her knees in defeat. She held her head in her hands and cried tears of anger and sadness.

Little Safflower flew close to her ear and rested beside her cheek. "Don't cry, Amberly. There's always a way out of every situation."

"It's no use, Safflower. It's over," Amberly said with a sigh.

Safflower suddenly flew in front of Amberly's face. "Don't say that! It's not over, Amberly! There's always a rainbow after every storm! There's always a light at the end of the tunnel!"

Suddenly, to Safflower's surprise, a bright, silvery-white light began to creep its way out from beneath a nearby chamber door on the other side of the corridor.

Startled, Amberly too noticed the bright light moving across the floor toward her.

"It's a light!" There's your light at the end of the tunnel, Amberly!" shouted Safflower. Then the light seemed to pull itself backward toward the door it had come from and just as quickly as it had appeared, it vanished.

"Light? That must mean there's a window inside that chamber!" Amberly shouted.

Safflower held on tightly to Amberly's shoulder as Amberly raced to the door. Before Amberly could grasp the door's handle, though, the door slowly opened by itself. She walked inside the dingy, grey-stone walled chamber with Safflower still sitting on her shoulder. Tall bookshelves lined the walls, filled with books about every type of magic spell you could imagine. Boggart's collection of spell books was much bigger than her Uncle Orin's collection. How she missed her Uncle Orin at that moment.

In front of the chamber's window was a large mirror with a brassy frame. It had to be the most beautiful mirror Amberly had ever seen. A golden glow emanated from the mirror itself and its brightness reminded Amberly of Whimsical Land's warm sun that she so desperately missed.

She crept slowly toward the mirror while a peculiar white mist poured out of it and hovered over the floor. The thick mist floated toward Amberly as she walked forward with Safflower on her shoulder.

Then the mist faded and to Amberly's utter amazement, she saw several Whimsical fairies walking through a forest inside of the mirror! The fairies looked as if they were sleep walking aimlessly through the forest with a thick fog hovering at their feet.

Amberly called out to the fairies but they did not hear her. They just kept walking around as if they were in a trance-like state. They were like little fairy ghosts, unaware of where they were going.

Just then, Amberly's father, Foster, appeared from behind a tree inside the mirror. Amberly's heart pounded and she let out a loud gasp before calling out to him. "Father! Father!" she cried out. But he didn't seem to hear her. He just kept walking aimlessly inside the mirror. "Father!" Amberly cried out again as Safflower flew excitedly above her.

"Amberly, look! It's Nissa!" Safflower shouted.

To Amberly's surprise, her cousin Nissa was walking listlessly behind her father. "Nissa!" Amberly cried out. Suddenly, Amberly felt as though something was pulling her forward. It felt like a magical, magnetic force pulling her closer toward the mirror.

"No!" she cried out as she used all the strength in her legs to try and stand firmly on the ground. She leaned her body back as far as she could, but the strong, magnetic force just kept pulling her closer and closer.

"I said, no!" Amberly screamed so loud that the magnetic pull dissipated, and she stopped moving forward. She was just inches away from the mirror now and she gasped when she saw her father inside the mirror once again.

Just then, Onyx burst into the chamber with Boggart following behind her. "Amberly!"

"He has my father and my cousin, Nissa!" Amberly cried out. Onyx looked at the mirror and saw the fairies walking aimlessly in the mirror's reflection. Feeling like a pile of bricks were anchored in her stomach, Onyx stared at her Uncle Boggart in shock.

Boggart glared at Amberly as she stood in front the mirror, and she returned his glare with an icy stare. "What did you do? Bring him back! Bring him back!" she screamed. She scratched her nails on the shiny mirror, desperately trying to free her father from the mirror's prison.

Boggart flew at Amberly. But his quick flight across the chamber floor was interrupted when Onyx extended the palm of her hand

and released a silvery beam of magic light that made him freeze in the air. Boggart was completely livid by now, but he was forced upward toward the ceiling by Onyx's magic beam, causing his arms and legs to flail around angrily. He stopped moving as his back smashed up against the chamber's ceiling. With his arms and legs sprawled out against the ceiling, Boggart looked like a spider stuck in its own web.

"Use your strength to *break* the spell, Amberly!" Onyx cried.

"I can't!" Amberly shouted back.

"Yes, you can! I know you can!"

Use my strength? Break the spell? Amberly said to herself. She suddenly realized what Onyx was trying to tell her. She had to break the mirror to break the spell. She grabbed at the mirror's frame and tried to pry it from the wall. "It won't budge!" she screamed.

"No!" Boggart shouted as he somehow managed to break free from Onyx's magic hold on him. In a flash, he flew down toward Amberly, whose eyes widened at the sight of him hovering above her. With a fuming rage inside, Boggart reached for Amberly's wing brace and tried to yank it off her back.

A sudden, strong, forceful wind blew him up in the air again. "Boggart, no!" Onyx screamed as she held out her hand, emitted gusts of wind from her palm, and directed them toward Boggart. The winds morphed into a sparkly purple beam that surrounded Boggart, lifted him higher into the air, and thrust him against the chamber's ceiling once again.

He was so angry that he shook his fists and yelled at Onyx. "Put me down! I'm warning you, Onyx! Release me!"

But Onyx didn't listen. She was more concerned about Amberly, who was still struggling to pull the mirror from the wall.

"Ha! You will never be able to move that mirror!" shouted Boggart.

"Just watch me!" Amberly screamed at the top of her lungs as she gripped both sides of the shiny brass mirror. She took a deep breath and tore the mirror away from the stone wall.

She smiled victoriously until she heard Onyx scream at her, "Amberly! Look out!"

Boggart had emitted a magical blue beam from the palm of his hand, and aimed it right at Amberly's head. She ducked down, but the blue beam grazed the top of her head, causing her to fall to her knees. She struggled to hold onto the mirror without dropping it. Luckily, Safflower had been hiding safely beneath Amberly's hair.

Onyx fought back and shot a purple beam of light with her own magic, which threw Boggart against the wall, this time causing his blue magic beam to disappear. His body was frozen against the wall, despite his attempt to free himself from Onyx's magical hold on him.

"Use your strength, Amberly! Break the spell!" Onyx shouted while Amberly, despite her strength, was struggling to stand up. She still held the mirror in her hands while trying to ignore her pounding headache.

Boggart looked at Onyx and then at Amberly, who suddenly sported a defiant smile. She finally stood up straight and Boggart's eyes widened as he shook his fist at her.

"No!!" he screamed as he fell to the floor, finally breaking Onyx's magical beam's hold on him once more.

"Break it, Amberly!" Onyx shouted.

Boggart turned toward Onyx with a chilling stare. Standing near the chamber's wall, he stretched out his hand toward Onyx and emitted his blue magic beam right at her forehead. "Enough!" Boggart said as his magic beam hit Onyx, causing her to crash to the floor.

Luckily, Onyx fell on to the hip that her knapsack was not resting on. Buggles popped his head out of the knapsack and looked at her sadly. He desperately wanted to help Onyx. All he could do was hide back inside her little knapsack and stay alive for her because they were inseparable. Buggles knew that Onyx needed him just as much as he needed her.

"No!! What have you done?" Amberly's intense anger seemed to make her grow stronger. She held the mirror up high over her head.

To Amberly's surprise, Onyx's legs were beginning to fade.

"What are you doing to her? Leave her alone!" Amberly shouted as Onyx lay on the chamber's floor, unconscious.

"And ruin all the fun? Never!" said Boggart with an evil grin.

"Lift your spell on her Boggart or I will shatter this precious mirror of yours!" Amberly shouted.

"Dear sweet fairy child, If you do that, those pretty little eyes of yours will never see your father, again."

"I don't believe you!"

"What you saw were just images of the Whimsical fairies. They weren't real," Boggart said with a chuckle.

"You're lying! Where is my father? Take me to him or I'll break it. I swear!" Amberly hollered as she glanced over at Onyx, who was now struggling to get up off the floor even though her legs were beginning to fade.

"If you break that mirror, your father and all the other Whimsical fairies will be stuck in its reflection for all eternity!" shouted Boggart. His eyes turned into red orbs that were filled with rage.

"But why? Why my father? Why the Whimsicals?"

"Why the Whimsicals?" Boggart let out a hearty laugh. "Well, for their pixie dust, of course!" He pointed to the corner of the chamber where there was a shelf lined with little glass bottles. They were filled with every color of powdery fairy-wing dust one could imagine.

Amberly stared at the beautiful myriad of rainbow-colored powders shimmering in the soft light.

"Not only does Whimsical pixie dust make plants and flowers grow, but the precious powder that falls from those wings of yours makes my magic the strongest in the land!" Bogart said with a cackling laugh. "Now, once I mix the elements I knew my sweet Onyx would bring to me after I made the legs of that weak grandfather of hers vanish with my spell, I'll be the most powerful fairy in the universe!" He held out his hand and emitted a shiny-red beam of light from his palm right toward Amberly.

Frightened, Amberly quickly lowered the mirror in front of her face, causing the red beam to hit the mirror's glass. She frantically walked forward with all the strength she had in her legs, while shielding her face with the mirror. As she walked toward Boggart, the red beam intensified.

Safflower held on tightly to Amberly's hair and snuggled close to her neck. "Be careful! I know you can do it!" she shouted into Amberly's ear.

The sound of howling wind filled the chamber and the hot, red beam of light emanating from the mirror suddenly pierced right through Boggart's body. He let out a loud cry, and exploded into one hundred little bubbles! The mix of Boggart's purple wings and the red light beam turned the floating bubbles into a beautiful magenta color.

The bright, reddish-purple bubbles reminded Amberly of the magnificent colors that existed in Whimsical Land. But her sweet thoughts of home were interrupted as the red ray of light abruptly disappeared and she fell forward. She landed flat on top of the mirror, cracking it into several pieces.

Buggles popped his head out of Onyx's knapsack, which was still lying next to her. Then he dove right back in to dodge a shard of glass that whizzed right by his head.

"Father!" Amberly cried out as she stared at the shards of glass now scattered on the floor. She wept softly as she moved the little pieces of mirror into a pile wishing that she could somehow put the mirror back together.

Safflower flew above Amberly's head. "Amberly, it's going to be ok. We just need to get out of here, now. There has to be another way. Your father wasn't really in that mirror! We have to search the Dark Forest!"

Amberly didn't seem to hear a word Safflower was saying. She noticed Onyx still lying in the corner groaning and holding her head. With Safflower back on her shoulder, holding on for dear life, Amberly rushed to Onyx's side. "Onyx!" she cried out and took Onyx's head onto her lap.

"Did you break it? Did you break the spell?" Onyx asked with a raspy, weak voice.

"I...I don't know if I broke the spell! The mirror shattered and I don't see my father or the others anymore!" Amberly shouted.

Onyx closed her eyes again and her arms suddenly vanished.

"Onyx! Please don't disappear!" shouted Amberly. "I'm so sorry I didn't believe that you were trying to help me! What do I do?"

Without Amberly and Onyx noticing, the magenta bubbles that had been floating in a corner of the ceiling were now forming into one big blob of connected bubbles and slowly morphing back into the shape of Boggart's body.

Within seconds, Boggart's body was intact and there was a kind of fury in his eyes. "You're going to pay for this!" he shouted. With great speed he flew right toward Amberly, who was still on her knees beside Onyx.

As he landed right in front her, Amberly jumped to her feet. With a stern look she faced him, holding out her scimitar sword the way her Uncle Orin had taught her. Boggart unleashed a blue lightning bolt from the palm of his hand. On impact, it knocked Amberly's sword right out of her grip. Amberly let out an angry snarl as her sword flew across the chamber. When it crashed on the stone floor the metal clanged so loudly that it hurt her ears.

Feeling vulnerable, Amberly crouched back down beside Onyx on the floor. Safflower let out a tiny scream as she hunkered down farther into Amberly's neck and beneath her red hair. Buggles tried to pull himself out of Onyx's knapsack but Amberly pushed him back down. "Stay there," she whispered as Boggart flew closer.

"Now you will never see your father again!" Boggart shouted at Amberly, and she glanced sadly at the shattered mirror on the floor. Then, with a wave of his arm, Boggart unleashed a blue lightning bolt that headed directly for Amberly's face.

"No!" she shouted. She jumped to her feet and leapt to the side, away from Onyx while trying to dodge the blue lightning bolt. The hot blue lightning bolt hit Amberly's wing brace, causing it to crack and fall off Amberly's back, exposing her tiny paralyzed wing. "No!!" she shouted again, as she lost her balance and fell, landing on her disabled wing.

Boggart let out a boisterous, evil laugh. He moved in closer to Amberly and kneeled in front of her as she began to cry in defeat.

The only thing Onyx could do was shudder in fear. She couldn't move or speak as she lay helplessly on the cold, stone floor.

"Oh, you poor thing you," said Boggart as he stared at Amberly. "You can't even fly or stand. What a waste of a perfectly good fairy." He clicked his tongue and shook his head.

Something inside of Amberly snapped. It was like an inner magic exploded inside of her and she stopped crying. She locked eyes with Boggart and took a deep breath. She wiped her own tears off her cheeks while Safflower flew inside of her sleeve.

A strange thing happened. Amberly began to feel something inside of her that she had never felt before. It was a warm feeling. It made her want to protect herself and her imperfections. She realized her own uniqueness made her who she really wanted to be— a fairy warrior.

As Boggart glared into Amberly's eyes with disdain, she began to see what her sister and Onyx appreciated about her—the value of her strength and how it could be used. Not only did she suddenly value and appreciate the strength in her arms and legs, but she understood she had a strong mind that could get her through anything, so long as she used the strength she'd been born with.

"I am not a waste!" Amberly shouted. She leapt in the air with lightning speed and kicked Boggart in the face with all her might.

Amberly's boot hit Boggart so hard that he was thrown all the way to the back of the chamber. His body slammed up against his tall bookshelf before he fell hard onto the stone floor.

As Boggart lay on the stone floor unconscious, with a few books that had fallen from one of the shelves resting on his stomach, Amberly landed back on her feet. But she lost her balance and toppled over.

"Amberly! Are you hurt?" Safflower shouted from inside Amberly's sleeve.

"I'm ok, Safflower," said Amberly. She tried to walk back toward Onyx, but with no success. After falling to the floor, she decided she'd best crawl the rest of the way.

Onyx was moaning and tears were streaming down her cheeks.

"It's going to be ok, Onyx. I promise. I'm going to get you out of here," Amberly said. She crawled over to where her cracked wing brace was lying in the corner.

Safflower jumped out of Amberly's sleeve, helped tie the wing brace back together, and then tied it onto Amberly's left shoulder with the leftover thread in Amberly's satchel.

With her wing brace secure on her back, Amberly stood up and ran to the corner of the chamber, picked up her sword, placed it in her scabbard, and then ran back to Onyx.

Onyx's arms had fully vanished now, and her legs were beginning to vanish as well. Amberly stroked her hair as the poor fairy slipped in and out of consciousness.

Chapter Twenty-One

What seemed like hours later, Amberly was still by Onyx's side on the chamber floor. Boggart was still unconscious and all Amberly could do was try and think of an escape plan.

Then something strange happened. Right in front of Amberly's eyes, several tiny, rainbow-colored balls of light shot out from the pile of broken mirror shards. The little balls of light swirled around Amberly and Onyx, and then surrounded the area where Onyx's arms and legs should have been with a soft, rainbow-colored glow. Amazingly, Onyx's arms and legs began to reappear!

"Onyx! Onyx look!" Amberly cried.

Onyx fluttered her eyes open and saw that her arms and legs were beginning to reappear. She smiled and a squeal of joy escaped her lips. Buggles popped his head out of Onyx's satchel and belted out little chitters of joy!

At that moment, the chamber door burst open and in flew Orion, Onyx's grandfather, on a golden chariot pulled by dragonflies. He flew right past Boggart, who was still unconscious on the floor. Orion's large, grey and purple wings fluttered quickly and his long white beard flew side to side caused by the chariot's bumpy landing as he pulled up.

Orion's legs were completely vanished and so was his left arm, but he still had his strong right arm to steer his dragonflies with their tiny, narrow, leather reins.

"Grandfather!" Onyx cried.

Orion quickly parked the chariot next to Onyx, whose arms and legs were now completely back to normal. The swirling balls of colorful lights flew over to him and surrounded the area where his legs and left arm should have been. Suddenly, his legs and arm became visible.

Amberly smiled at Onyx and hugged her with a sigh of relief while Safflower flew happily above them.

Onyx giggled at Amberly's sudden burst of affection and loved every minute of the attention. She pulled Buggles out of her knapsack and kissed him.

Suddenly, the colorful little balls of light began to magically turn into the Whimsical fairies who had been trapped in the mirror.

Onyx noticed the beautiful fairies fluttering above them. Their vibrant colors almost blinded her in the dimly lit chamber. "Amberly, look!" she shouted. She pointed up toward the gorgeous fairies.

Amberly looked up and smiled from ear to ear. "Whenever two or more Whimsical fairies gather together with good intentions, they are able to break any evil spell there may be!" she said.

Onyx looked at her arms, which were now completely back to normal, and sighed in relief. Her grandfather jumped out of his chariot and hugged her tightly.

Amberly watched them hug, and tears welled up in her eyes. How she longed for her family. She would have given anything to have her father back, but she was happy for Onyx. After all, Amberly wasn't the only one who had known suffering. She rushed over to Orion and Onyx and hugged them. Safflower sat on her shoulder and sighed a sigh of relief.

Amberly took a long deep breath and closed her eyes. Tears rolled down her cheeks and a million thoughts of home and her father raced through her head while the Whimsical fairies flew above them and hugged each other. They were so happy to be out of that ridiculous mirror.

Amberly opened her eyes and looked up at the happy fairies chatting and hugging as they fluttered up high near the chamber's ceiling.

She expected nothing more that could add to the beautiful sight…
until she saw her missing cousin, Nissa fluttering above her. "Nissa!
Is it really you?"

"Amberly!" Nissa flew down and gave Amberly the tightest hug.

"I thought I was never going to see you again!" said Amberly as
she hugged her cousin back. "I've missed you so much."

Onyx's eyes widened and she motioned for Amberly to turn
around. "Amberly! Amberly, look!" she squealed with delight.

Amberly let go of Nissa, spun herself around in a flash, and there
she saw him. Standing with his bright, red-orange wings and red hair
stood Foster, her father. The two stared at each other in disbelief.

"Father?" she said softly.

"Amberly? Is that you?" he said with a smile. He couldn't believe
how much she had grown.

"Father!!" Amberly screamed. She ran toward Foster and he lifted
his fairy daughter up with his strong arms and hugged her close. He
hugged her so tightly that she could hardly breathe, but she didn't
care. All she cared about was that she had finally found her father.

"Oh, I've missed you so much," Foster said to Amberly quietly.
He slowly set her down and stared at her as she smiled back at him
with her eyes sparkling like little green gems.

"What a beautiful young fairy you've grown up to be. I can't believe
you're already twelve fairy years old now!"

"Wow, you remembered my birthday!"

"I never stopped counting the days," said Foster.

Listening to Amberly and her father's conversation, Onyx and
Orion were smiling from ear to ear. Onyx put her head on her grandfather's shoulder. She was overjoyed both about her grandfather's
recovery and the fact that Amberly had finally found her father. She
knew that this beautiful moment would never be forgotten.

The moment was interrupted by more balls of colorful light that
abruptly shot out of the broken mirror pieces once again. They flew
straight into the air and created a large, gaping hole in the chamber's

ceiling. The loud, crashing sound of the chamber's ceiling busting open caused Boggart to stir. His arms began to twitch, and his head moved from side to side as he tried to wake himself.

The rainbow-colored balls of light flew steadily through the hole in the ceiling toward a brightly-lit patch of blue sky that had formed in the middle of the Dark Forest's sky. Amberly gasped.

"Amberly! Foster! Hurry, we must go!" Nissa shouted and then flew through the gaping hole in the ceiling with the other whimsical fairies.

Suddenly, a piece of the chamber's ceiling broke lose and almost fell on top of Onyx but she snapped out of her trance just in time for her grandfather and her to move out of the way.

"What's happening?" Amberly yelled, covering her ears with her hands.

The ground began to shake, rumble, and sway, and one of the chamber's stone walls collapsed.

The collapsed wall exposed more of the Dark Forest's cold outdoors and the ground suddenly stopped shaking. They could see miles and miles of the quiet Dark Forest's sky lit up by a row of rainbow-colored balls of light headed straight for a patch of blue sky that looked as if it were floating in the middle of the Dark Forest's sky.

Within the patch of blue sky, were small, fluffy white clouds. Amberly and her father stared at it and suddenly felt a glimmer of hope. Could the beautiful patch blue sky be a part of Whimsical Land's sky? Amberly wondered with excitement.

One by one, newly freed Whimsical fairies began flying through the large hole in the chamber's wall. Some flew through the gaping hole in the ceiling and they all followed the row of colorful lights that floated toward the crystal-blue patch of sky.

Chapter Twenty-Two

By this time, Whimsical Land was buzzing with some excitement of its own. The ground had been shaking ferociously there as well, while Amberly's entire fairy village, including Calista and her mother, had been searching the entire forest for her.

As the ground in Whimsical Land began to shake, pebbles resting next to an abandoned wolf's den that little Bliss, Corliss, and Remi had been exploring during their search for Amberly, had toppled down into the den's entrance. The little whimsies were trapped inside.

Avery and a few other teen fairies, along with the trapped whimsies' parents, had been desperately trying to move each heavy pebble as quickly as they could, away from the little den's opening. Just as they removed the last pebble away from the wolf den's entrance, Bliss, Corliss, and Remi flew out directly into their parents' arms and hugged them. But then little Remi broke away from his fairy mother's hug and shouted, "Look!"

To all the Whimsical fairies' surprise, Remi was pointing to a large, gaping hole in the ground a few feet away from them. Every Whimsical fairy that had been searching for Amberly flew to the open trench in the ground. They saw the vastly large Dark Forest miles below while the rainbow-colored balls of light began rising toward them. The colorful balls of light suddenly popped up out of the large trench onto Whimsical Land's ground and morphed back into the Whimsical fairies that had been lost.

"Amberly? Avery yelled into the open trench in the ground, as the other fairies hugged their loved ones that had been lost for several years.

"Amberly!" the whimsies shouted down into the open trench in the ground that lead to the Dark Forest below them.

"Amberly! Where are you?" Spice shouted.

"But, she can't fly..." said Avery sadly as he looked down into the gaping hole. The little whimsies looked up at Avery and tried to hold back their tears.

Back in Boggart's half-destroyed chamber, Amberly, her father, Onyx, and her grandfather could hear the whimsies calling Amberly's name.

"Do you hear that?" said Onyx with a tear in her eye and a big smile.

"Come with us, Onyx! You and your grandfather! I know you would love Whimsical Land!" said Amberly. She held both Onyx's hands in her own and the two spry little fairies grinned from ear to ear. Foster looked on with concern and Onyx's grandfather shook his head no.

Onyx turned around and looked at her grandfather, who to her disappointment was sporting a very large frown. "No, Onyx, my sweet fairy. We belong here in the Dark Forest."

"But Grandfather, what if..."

"Enough," her grandfather interrupted. "It's too dangerous to move in between realms."

"But, just for a little while and then we'll come back!" Onyx said with a sparkle of hope in her voice.

"No, the gateway to Whimsical Land may close at any time. We must not keep them any longer."

Onyx and Amberly looked at each other sadly as they held hands.

"Amberly, he is right. We must go now," said Foster.

"But when will I see Onyx again, Father?" Foster and Onyx's grandfather looked at their young fairies sadly while Onyx and Amberly hugged and cried together.

Safflower flew over to Buggles, whose head was peeking out of Onyx's knapsack. She gave him a kiss. "Goodbye, Buggles," she said sweetly while a funny chirping sound escaped from Buggles' mouth. Safflower smiled and then quickly flew back to Amberly's shoulder.

Onyx pulled away from Amberly's embrace and wiped her eyes. She pulled two magic stones from her knapsack and handed one to Amberly. "Here, take this. Whenever you want to talk to me, just stare at this stone and think of me and my image will appear on the stone. We can communicate with our thoughts."

Amberly hugged Onyx tightly. "Thank you. I'll never forget you, Onyx."

"They're waiting for us, Amberly," said Foster. Amberly nodded her head and took her father's hand in her own. With one swoop, he lifted her up and swung her on to his back.

"Goodbye, Amberly! Bye, Amberly's father!" shouted Onyx as she waved. Amberly and Foster waved back at Onyx and her grandfather. With that, Foster flew through the hole in Boggart's chamber wall and followed the line of rainbow-colored balls of light, heading straight for Whimsical Land's patch of bright-blue sky shining brightly in the midst of the Dark Forest's murky grey sky.

As Foster flew alongside the row of colorful balls of lights, the little fanciful orbs began making sudden popping sounds. All at once, the colorful balls of lights morphed into beautiful Whimsical fairies. Vibrant wings in various colors of blue, purple, teal, red, yellow, green, and orange lit up the grey sky until one by one they all entered the blue patch of sky that led to the open trench in Whimsical Land's ground.

Foster and Amberly were the last to pop up through the open trench in Whimsical Land's mossy earth and they flew high above the happy Whimsical fairies who were excitedly calling out Amberly's and Foster's names. At that moment, Foster saw his wife, Orla, and his other fairy daughter, Calista, waving to him. With Amberly still on his back, he flew down to the ground like a fierce hawk, and he landed right next to them.

Laughing and crying at the same time, Orla and Calista rushed toward Amberly and Foster. The four became locked in a fairy embrace while Safflower flew happily above them.

Amberly felt as though she were in a dream! It was finally over. Her father was home!

"Amberly, Amberly!" the little whimsies screamed as they happily flew with Avery and Spice toward Amberly's reunited family.

Meanwhile, Whimsical fairy musicians began to play festive music to honor all the Whimsical fairies that were finally back home. Before long, every fairy was dancing around Amberly and her family.

Chapter Twenty-Three

Back in the Dark Forest, Onyx and her grandfather were still staring up at the blue patch of sky through the gaping hole in the chamber room's ceiling. Suddenly, Boggart awoke from his unconscious slumber and belted out the evilest of laughs. Onyx and her grandfather turned around and saw him standing behind them, looking up through the gashed-out ceiling.

"Could it be?" Boggart shouted as he squinted his eyes at the light-blue patch of sky in the middle of the darkness. "Could that be the entrance to Whimsical Land? Oh, this is too easy!"

Onyx glared at Boggart and gasped. "No…" she said to herself. She could not let Boggart hurt Amberly and her family. But in a matter of seconds, Boggart flew through the opened ceiling and up into the sky.

"Boggart, no!!" Onyx's grandfather yelled. He and Onyx quickly jumped into his dragonfly chariot and followed right behind Boggart, whose evil, cackling laugh echoed through the dark sky.

The chariot was right at Boggart's heels and just as Boggart reached the opening in sky that led to Whimsical Land, Onyx stood up, grabbed his foot, and held on for dear life. She had her own feet wedged beneath the chariot's seat so that she wouldn't get pulled out.

"Arg!" Boggart shouted as he tried to shake Onyx off his foot. Onyx continued to hold on tightly, but the force of him trying to pull himself from her grip caused her foot to unwedge from beneath the chariot's seat.

"Onyx!" her grandfather screamed as he grabbed on to her flailing foot and held on tight while he steered the chariot with his other hand.

Boggart finally made it to the mossy open trench in Whimsical Land's ground and pulled himself up while Onyx still held on to his foot.

"Enough!" he yelled. He turned over onto his back and shot out a blue magic beam from the palm of his hand right at Onyx and her grandfather. The strong force of Boggart's magical beam made Onyx, her grandfather and the chariot fly into a nearby bush. Boggart flew as fast as he could in the opposite direction toward a large weeping willow tree next to the open trench.

Though Boggart flew in a hurry, so as not to be seen by the Whimsical fairies, one fairy toddler in her mother's arms spotted him in an instant. "Mama, look!" she shouted as she pointed to the weeping willow tree just as Boggart flew into its hollow trunk. Boggart was nowhere to be seen now and the little whimsy toddler's mother just continued to dance in the large circle with all the other dancing Whimsical fairies.

Amberly and Calista were the only ones not dancing to the spritely music, because they were so busy watching their happy fairy parents dance. They turned away and giggled when they saw their fairy parents kiss.

A few feet away from the happy Whimsical fairies was the bush that Onyx and her grandfather had landed in. The dragonflies that pulled the chariot were lying in the bushes behind them.

Onyx and her grandfather peered out from the bush's foliage and watched the colorful Whimsical fairies dance. Onyx's grandfather looked on with a worried stare but not Onyx. No, Onyx wasn't worried at all. Instead, she smiled so wide she thought her cheekbones were going to shatter. Her heart leapt with a joy she had never felt before and she thought that she could live in this colorful place forever.

Her eyes widened as she watched Amberly and her family and all the other Whimsical fairies dance with joy in the distance. She suddenly forgot all about the Dark Forest and where she had come from. She wasn't worried about what would happen next in this strange land and all was well within her fairy heart and soul.

Acknowledgement

When I first started writing *Amberly and the Secret of the Fairy Warriors,* I knew I wanted to inspire young girls to believe in their own uniqueness and strength. Little did I know that by writing this story, I would come to appreciate my own inner strength and resilience, as well!

I could not have finished this book without the love and support of my family, friends, and coworkers. I cannot thank you all enough for listening to me endlessly talk about Amberly--over the years, as I wrote and rewrote her story.

I am especially grateful to Earl Martin, my coworker and friend, who created the initial concept design for the book cover. Earl, your encouragement, and enthusiasm meant the world to me. I will be forever grateful for the time and effort you spent creating a visual representation of these characters that lived in my imagination for so long.

Also, a huge "Thank You" to my wonderful editor, Rhonda Hayter, for believing in this book! Rhonda, your keen eye and expert knowledge of the craft of storytelling was a godsend. Your encouraging words and enthusiasm for Amberly's story helped to bring her--and this book--to life. For that, I am eternally grateful!

Writing a work of fiction can be a long, and tedious process, which I could not have completed without the unwavering love and encouragement of *My Love. Honey, you will forever be my muse!*

About The Author

Gina Vallance has an AA degree in child development and a BA in English. She has worked as a preschool teacher and also as an art activity facilitator in a courthouse's children's waiting room. A childhood illness that sometimes left her marginalized and bullied was the inspiration for Amberly, a fairy who refuses to be sidelined by her disability. Gina works in Social Services in Los Angeles County and is happily married to her soulmate. They have a Shorkie dog named Emma, a Malshi dog named Raffaele, and two feline sisters named Belle and Jasmine. The next book in Gina's series, Onyx, is on the way.